AIRSTREAM

AIRSTREAM

Patricia Young

STORIES

BIBLIOASIS

FIRST EDITION
SECOND PRINTING: October 2006

Library and Archives Canada Cataloguing in Publication

Young, Patricia, 1954–
Airstream / Patricia Young.

1-897231-02-4 (HAND CASED)
1-897231-01-6 (PBK.)

I. Title.
PS8597.067A65 2006   C813'.54   C2006-901947-9

Cover image adapted from the painting:
"Airstream" by DEBORAH ANGUS
20 x 24 inches, oil

Readied for the press by
JOHN METCALF

We acknowledge the support of the Canada Council
for the Arts for our publishing program.

 Canada Council   Conseil des Arts
for the Arts   du Canada

PRINTED AND BOUND IN CANADA

for Clea

Stories

DUMB FISH

You'd like that wouldn't you?" Darlene's mother says. "You and me diving for abalone and gooey ducks?" Darlene and her mother are standing on the veranda, mixing jars of paint at the rickety worktable. Cock-a-Beauty and Sweetheart-Heart cluck around their feet, waiting for Darlene to throw a handful of seeds. "All the girls on Cheju-do grew up to be divers," her mother says. "They were different from normal women."

Darlene imagines swimming in the coral reefs, opening and closing her mouth, her hair streaming out behind, arms dissolving into fins.

"Rrribbit," she says.

"You win," her mother says and plugs in the coloured lanterns strung along the eaves. The veranda lights up like a Christmas tree.

*

WHILE DARLENE'S FATHER is at work her mother invents projects. She and Darlene roll out pastry, and then fill their pies with whatever's in the fridge — peaches, jam, onions. They feed the wood stove until the oven's five hundred degrees. Darlene's mother wears a bikini and sweat runs down her face. She says it's like a Turkish prison in the kitchen.

"Don't you think, Darlene, don't you think it's like a Turkish prison?"

Or they collect wildflowers to press into books, each day wandering deeper into the forest for Shooting Stars and Indian Paintbrush. Darlene's mother holds Darlene close to her side, looking over her shoulder for wild animals, even though Darlene's father has told her again and again the woods are benign.

Benign, Darlene knows, means no cougars, no bears.

Today Darlene and her mother are making cardboard fish to hang from the bathroom ceiling. Exotic fish, the kind Darlene saw in the aquarium at the doctor's office. It's been a hot dry summer and every day she and her mother wake to the sweet smell of burning forest. Still in pyjamas, they sit on the veranda and turn on the radio. They listen to reports of water-bombing and dip their brushes into jars of pink and yellow and turquoise. They hear of towns being evacuated farther up the coast and push needle and thread through a dorsal fin.

*

"COULD THEY BREATHE underwater?" Darlene asks. She's painting a fuzzy chick on the side of her fish. She wants her mother to tell her more about the haenyo divers. Darlene likes it when her mother talks. Sometimes she's silent for hours and hours. On those days, Darlene wriggles underneath the barn and lies on her back. Time is huge and green and passes through her slowly. The wind might be blowing, the treetops thrashing wildly back and forth, but down on the ground Darlene can hear a cricket's legs move in the grass.

"They could stay underwater for twenty minutes," her mother says. "It was long ago. Those divers belonged to an ancient tribe." She stops stirring paint and presses her palms against an invisible pane of glass. What is she looking at? Can she see something out there, moving in the woods?

"Remember, they didn't have wet suits or goggles," Darlene's mother says. "Just their arms and legs and lungs."

Darlene follows her mother's gaze. A diver swimming in and out of the trees, fish tail flicking light and shadow?

"Deer," Darlene's mother says and breathes again.

"Just a deer," Darlene agrees.

"Women have an extra layer of fat," her mother says, "so they could stand the cold."

Darlene curls forward, trying to make a stomach roll, something to grab onto.

"They'd surface just long enough to exhale and make a long whistling sound," her mother says. "They'd do it all day. Come up for air and dive back down."

"Can you hold your breath for twenty minutes?" Darlene asks. "Do you have an extra layer of fat?"

*

DARLENE'S FATHER LIKES to tell how Darlene's mother was slinging beer at the Six Mile House the night he walked in. At thirty-two he was still moving from town to town and job to job but when he saw Darlene's mother in jeans and cowboy boots, her long braids and hand held high, balancing a tray of glasses, he stopped. He sat on a stool at the bar and watched as she took money from the loud and sweaty truckers and loggers. She appeared aloof and self-possessed and made no attempt to ingratiate herself with the customers the way the other waitresses did. All night she wove, unsmiling, in and out of the little tables and at the end of her shift he went over and introduced himself, then offered to buy her a meal next door at Ian's All-Night Café.

When Darlene was four her mother decided she wanted a fresh start, to begin a new kind of life, and she persuaded her father to buy this land in the forest and live in the barn, the only structure still standing on the property. A pioneer farmer had built it around the beginning of the last century. Darlene's father added a bathroom, a loft, and an old fashioned veranda which, her mother says, makes the place look a bit like a derelict southern mansion. He also sawed holes in the walls and caulked in tall windows he'd salvaged from demolished houses. But the rooms are still dark. Even after the trees came down Darlene would stand in the kitchen and lift her face to the single ray of light filtering through the massive trunks.

Darlene's father drove two miles down the road to introduce himself to the Lamonts after he and Darlene and her mother had settled in, and Mrs. Lamont gave him a tour of the house and gardens. The Lamonts travelled for most of the year but in July they always returned to the house they'd built on their private lake.

"Drug money," Darlene's father said when he came back.

"Why do you say that?" her mother asked.

"The place is obscene," he said. "All the granite and black marble. Staircases going nowhere. The landscaping alone must have cost a small fortune. It looks like the eighth wonder of the world down there. And the best part is, neither of them seems to have a job. Nice people, though. From California. Real nice."

"People are many things," Darlene's mother said, "but nice is not one of them."

She stood at the window and looked out at the forest which hung like a heavy green curtain on the other side of the glass. "What would it be like to live in a lighthouse?" she said, and Darlene's father put down the newspaper he was reading and folded it in his lap.

"Hold on there," he said. "You already have a barn."

"Imagine waking up at the edge of the world," Darlene's mother said." Just the ocean in front of you. Nothing in your way. Nothing to block your view."

*

DARLENE'S MOTHER'S long toes curl around the edge of the bathtub as she stands and reaches up with one hand to push a thumbtack into the ceiling. One after another, she attaches the long threads at the end of which dangle Darlene's fish.

In the kitchen, preparing Darlene's favourite dinner — toast, roasted garlic and pitted olives — her mother looks around and says, "This room could use some fish too." Darlene and her mother sit at the table and fit the olives on the tips of their fingers then pull them off slowly with their teeth. After Darlene's eaten her fingertips, she asks her mother how many more fish they need.

"Enough for all the rooms," she says and makes a long whistling sound.

The well is low at this time of year, so Darlene's mother runs only a few inches of water in the tub and then lights a kerosene lamp. Darlene lies back and watches the fish, suspended above her, swaying slightly in the air currents. Drying Darlene off with a towel, her mother talks about the Chinese folk tale that says lots of fish in a house mean good luck. "Fish protect people," she says.

"But our fish aren't alive," Darlene says. "They're made of cardboard."

Darlene's mother looks at Darlene for the first time in days. "For a child," she says, "you are very literal-minded."

She bathes next and when she's finished she scoops Darlene up and dances her around the barn to Willie Nelson on the radio. *Georgia, Georgia*, he sings. *An old sweet song.* As they pass through the bathroom, Darlene closes her eyes and the fish lightly touch her face.

*

IT'S PAST ELEVEN when Darlene's father arrives home, his skin black, his jeans and T-shirt stinking of smoke. Early that morning he left for work to hack hiking trails through a provincial park, but men from the Ministry of Forests took him and his crew off the job to help fight the fire. They were flown up the island in a helicopter where they dug ditches until they couldn't see the shovels in front of their faces. Now he sits on the icebox and pulls off his boots. Darlene's mother walks carefully across the room trying not to spill the beer she has poured for him. She doesn't cook, but when Darlene's father gets home from work she always brings him a beer in one of the gold-rimmed glasses the gas station on the highway was giving away free with every full tank of gas.

The next morning Darlene wakes to silence. She makes her way down the loft steps and out to the veranda, and there's her mother, not far from the barn, sitting on a stump that's round as a dinner table. The winter before she begged Darlene's father to take down some of the fir trees.

She was afraid lightning would strike.

She was afraid their roots were rotten.

She was afraid the trees were leaning toward the barn.

She was afraid a storm would blow one down and crush the family while they slept.

"No," Darlene's father said. "They're hundreds of years old. I won't do it."

But Darlene's mother couldn't sleep worrying about the trees, and she began to wander at night. Darlene could hear her struggling with the lid on her bottle of pills. She'd run the tap to cover the sound, but Darlene could still hear the little rattling sound. Her parents fought

15

over those pills, her mother saying she needed them, her father saying they'd make anyone crazy. Once, her father emptied a bottle into the toilet while Darlene's mother wept. If he knew what she'd been through, she said, he wouldn't be so heartless.

Darlene's father left a magazine article open on her mother's dresser. It was about a woman in California who'd lived for two years in an ancient redwood tree to protest against logging. People called her Butterfly Woman because she liked it up there, swaying in the mist-shrouded treetops. Darlene's mother read the article but the night wandering didn't stop. The wind funnelled down through the valley and huge branches scraped against the walls and tin roof. Darlene would wake to the sound of her mother making her way down the stairs to boil water for tea. She'd fiddle with the radio dial and when she found the country station she'd turn it down low. That's how Darlene would find her in the morning, head on the table, asleep.

And then Darlene and her mother went away for a few days to stay at the Cherry Bend Motel. When they got back six fir trees lay sprawled on the ground like felled giants. Darlene's mother acted as though nothing were different but her body seemed forlorn, as though it couldn't bear the weight of itself.

Darlene didn't like to think of the terrible thing that had happened while she and her mother had been at the motel playing Go Fish with the deck of cards they'd found in a drawer. She didn't like to think about her father's friend, the faller, approaching the trees with his huge chainsaw. The blade biting into the bark, slicing through wood. Darlene imagined the other trees watching, whispering, *murderer. Murderer.*

For months her parents climbed around and over the fallen trees, but she didn't hear her mother or father speak about them. It was as though the trees weren't there. It was as though their spirits had left for some other place.

*

THIS MORNING the chickens sit next to Darlene's mother on the stump, wings and heads pulled in. She's also holding her knees close to her chest. The forest is deathly quiet, the trees and animals and insects bracing themselves the way they do just before an earthquake. The cloudless sky is a deep smoky blue.

"More fish?" Darlene's mother says, but Darlene is bored with her mother's latest project. It's like Christmas, when there were too many gingerbread men to decorate, or Easter when she boiled too many eggs. Her mother leaps down from the stump to join Darlene on the veranda.

"Dumb fish," she says.

"Don't say that, Darlene," her mother says.

"Dumb, *dumb* fish," Darlene says, then goes inside and puts on the same things she puts on every day: a white undershirt, gumboots, and her favourite skirt with the elastic waistband.

"That skirt needs to be washed," her mother says when Darlene comes back out, but she doesn't make Darlene take it off. It has blue and red pleats, and when Darlene twirls the colours spin into orange.

After breakfast she slaps paint on the fish her mother has cut out of mouldy cardboard she found in the shed. Cock-a-Beauty and Sweetheart-Heart walk all over the table, their feet making prints on the wet fish lying on their sides. Darlene tells her mother she doesn't care anymore if the fish are pretty or happy or dangle in flocks.

"Schools," her mother says, looking at the sky. "Fish swim in schools."

*

NOT LONG AFTER the trees came down Darlene's mother noticed carpenter ants chewing up a soft corner of the kitchen floor. Darlene listened while her mother talked on the phone to an exterminator from the Yellow Pages. Her voice was low and troubled as though she were still arguing with Darlene's father about chopping down the trees.

"White leghorns," she said a few days later when she returned with two chicks. "They eat ants." She wrapped the chicks in a dishtowel and gave them to Darlene. "They're yours. You can name them."

After that, Darlene carried Cock-a-Beauty and Sweetheart-Heart in an old biscuit tin, and when the chicks grew bigger, they followed her everywhere, down to the fallen trees where she liked to pull thick chunks of bark off the trunks. One day, on her way to the compost, Darlene's mother stopped to explain the trees' growth to Darlene. She pointed to a wide light-coloured ring and told Darlene it meant the weather had been warm and wet that year. She pointed to a dark narrow ring and said it meant cold and dry. While her mother became engrossed in counting the rings, Darlene pulled a piece of bark off the tree, exposing the wood bugs crawling underneath. She touched one with her finger and it curled into a ball. She tried to feed the ball to one of her chicks. She was so absorbed in the wood bugs and chicks she was startled to hear her mother's voice.

"Five hundred and thirty-three."

"What?" Darlene said.

"Years," her mother said. "Five hundred and thirty-three years old."

Darlene watched her mother start down the hill with the compost bucket. The flattened grass was as slippery as ice and she fell. For a long time she just sat there, staring at the forest, eggshells and spinach and orange rinds mushed over her legs.

*

SOMETIME IN THE EVERNING, Darlene and her mother feel the earth vibrate. The vibrations grow stronger and eventually a car passes the barn.

"Sounds different," her mother says. "The Lamonts must have bought a new vehicle."

Darlene is peeling the skin from an apple with her fingernail. It is difficult to do. "Car," she says when the vehicle passes, going the other way.

The vehicle reverses and turns around, and Darlene and her mother wait and listen, until a white jeep turns into their driveway and wends slowly through the trees. Below the veranda, a man in sandals and shorts gets out of the jeep and walks toward the barn.

"Think I'm lost," he says.

"Looks like," Darlene's mother says.

The man comes up the steps and onto the veranda. His shirt has many pockets and his hair is pulled back in an elastic band. "You live out here?" he asks.

"We do," Darlene's mother says.

"Far from the maddening crowd," he says, smiling at Darlene, then at her mother. On the front of her sundress is a big yellow sun that seems to swirl into her solar plexus. Earlier, she wrapped her braids around the top of her head but they've slipped to one side and now it appears she's wearing a skewed crown.

"Our phone's not working," Darlene's mother says.

This isn't true. It rang three times that day, although Darlene's mother refused to answer. She never answers, because, she says, it's always someone trying to sell her something she doesn't want, usually carpet cleaning services. When Darlene begs her mother to answer the ringing phone, her mother says, "Look around you, Darlene. Do you see any carpets?"

Darlene wishes her father were not away fighting the fire. He likes talking to people. He talks to them everywhere he and Darlene go. The last time they went into town he talked to a boy having trouble getting his motorcycle started, and then he talked for a long time to a woman selling raffle tickets outside the liquor store. Darlene's father would like this man, she is sure of it. He'd say, "Come in, sit down, have a beer." He'd take the map out of the flour canister and unfold it on the kitchen table. He'd show the man where he is and how to find his way again.

"My husband's at work," Darlene's mother says. "He'll be home soon."

Another lie.

"Could I ask for a bowl of water?" the man says, and nods toward the jeep. In the front seat a black dog is panting. "She's an old girl, can't walk too well. Arthritis in the back legs."

Darlene's mother takes Darlene firmly by the hand and they go into the barn and fill a cooking pot. When they return the man thanks them and carries the pot down to the jeep. Darlene watches him hold it steady while the dog laps up the water.

"Rrribbit," Darlene says. This is the third night in a row that she's heard the first frog.

Not taking her eyes off the jeep, her mother walks over and plugs in the coloured lanterns. The man comes back onto the veranda.

"I see you've been doing some logging," he says.

Darlene's mother shrugs.

Darlene likes the man with the thirsty old dog and hopes he'll stay. "Do you want to paint a fish?" she asks. Darlene's mother's face shows neither surprise nor anger, but it is a little of both. Darlene bites into the apple's messy brown pulp. "Look," she says and shows the man the fish she's just painted. "It's not my best. My best is hanging in the bathroom. It has chicks on both sides."

The man glances at Darlene's mother, and then follows Darlene into the barn, past the dangling fish, their big eyes and wide smiles. "There," Darlene says, pointing, "that one, it's my best."

"If you're looking for the Lamonts," Darlene's mother says from the doorway, her arms crossed, "you passed their gate. It's the one just before the road peters out."

"Wait a minute," the man says to Darlene. "Am I standing inside a barn? Are you the farmer's wife?"

Darlene says she's not married, she's only six, and her mother tells the man about the pioneer farmer who abandoned the homestead because of the rock and poor soil. On the veranda Darlene stands beside the man, watching over him as he paints thin curlicue lines on the side of his fish. When the paint dries he paints another design over top. He's going for a layered effect, he says, and when he's finished, he holds up his fish.

"Nice," Darlene says.

"What have you heard?" her mother asks. "About the fire?"

"They're saying rain," the man says, looking around, smiling as though everything he sees is remarkable — the tree trunks splayed like gigantic pick-up-sticks, the barn full of fish, the chickens huddled on the rickety table, Darlene's mother's skewed crown. Darlene leans over the veranda railing, trying to see the dog, now lying down in the back of the jeep.

"Hey dog," she says.

"Cody," the man says. "Name's Cody."

"Hey Cody," Darlene says. "Watch this." She twirls in her pleated skirt and when she gets dizzy she collapses on the outdoor sofa. She lies on her back listening to the man tell her mother he met the Lamonts the year before in Thailand.

"Loosely speaking," he says, "we're business partners."

"Ah," Darlene's mother says. "So that's how it is."

And then he's telling her about the hardwood forests being logged to death for their teak, and Darlene's mother asks what a teak tree looks like. The man says teak can grow as tall as firs and he describes their buttressed trunks and spreading crowns, their large drooping leaves and small white flowers.

"And the smell. The wood retains its fragrance for years."

Darlene closes her eyes and when she opens them it is dark and the man is alone on the veranda, his dog at his feet. The chickens are nowhere to be seen. Darlene sits up on the sofa and watches the man walk down the front steps, and there, standing on the rock sloping into the forest, is her mother. Darlene moves closer and though she can't see the trees she imagines them also leaning closer, trying to hear what her mother is saying.

"I thought this was what I wanted. Instead, I always feel trapped and afraid."

"What's to be afraid of?" the man says.

"And now this," Darlene's mother says. "It's like living in the middle of a graveyard."

The man says nothing.

"He did it for me but we both know these trees didn't have to come down."

"They're only trees," the man says.

"He blames me. He'd never admit it but he does."

The man says something that makes Darlene's mother laugh and then she seems to lift off the ground, her body levitating and stretching out horizontally. In slow motion, her feet push against the man's shoulder as though against the side of a pool, and then she's doing a kind of leisurely breaststroke, her legs kicking rhythmically. There's no moon, but Darlene can see the shape of her mother swimming away from her, into the darkness. Darlene's chest hurts as she leans over the veranda and tries to call her mother back — *Georgia, Georgia, an old sweet song* — but instead of words, air bubbles come out of her mouth.

*

DARLENE WAKES in her father's arms. Reeking of smoke, he carries her up to the loft and her little truckle bed. The next morning when she comes down, he's sitting at the kitchen table, arms and face still black. One hand's around a coffee mug, the other's holding a piece of paper.

"Your mother's gone," he says.

"Where?" Darlene asks.

"She said she'd phone as soon as she could."

Darlene doesn't know what else to ask so she climbs onto her father's lap and they sit and listen to the first drops of rain hit the tin roof.

Later that day, they drive into town for groceries and Darlene's school supplies. At Ian's Café they sit across from each other in a booth where she orders lemon meringue pie but after flattening the white peaks with her fork and squishing the yellow goo, she pushes the plate away. On the drive home her father asks if she's looking forward to grade one and she says, "Am I ever." He smiles and says it'll be good for Darlene to be around other kids.

That night her mother does phone. Her father speaks first, and then hands Darlene the receiver. She presses it against her ear but her mother's words are a jumble of sound that make no sense. After Darlene hangs up she can still see her mother's words scurrying around inside her head, bumping into each other like the wood bugs beneath the bark.

Over the next few months Darlene's mother calls from towns and cities up and down the coast, and one night in November when Darlene's in the kitchen scraping corn niblets off her plate for Cock-a-Beauty and Sweetheart-Heart, she hears her father in the next room. "You've got to stop this. It's hell on Darlene." After that there are no calls for a while, and then her mother forgets her promise and she phones when Darlene is in bed. "For Christ sake, do you have any idea what time it is?" her father says. "This isn't fair."

That winter Darlene spends a lot of time on the monkey bars in the schoolyard waiting for her father to pick her up on his way home from work. Hanging upside down from her knees, she rolls her eyes back and the woodchip playground becomes a sky. She flutters her eyelids and chants the new unlisted number, hoping her mother can hear her wherever she is. Gravity pulls the blood into Darlene's head and she remembers the August nights after her mother left and how she lay on her truckle bed listening to the fallen trees die and die again.

*

"AM I EVER," Darlene said to her father. When they arrived at the barn she ran up the steps ahead of him, expecting to see her mother walking around in her nightgown and cowboy boots, brushing her teeth. Darlene stood in the dark, holding onto her school supplies, and then her father dropped the bags of groceries on the kitchen table. He fumbled around, opening the warming oven, feeling for the box of matches. Darlene's pupils dilated and just before her father lifted the glass chimney to light the lamp, she saw bits of painted cardboard flicker like a swarm of fireflies above her head.

GIRL OF THE WEEK

*F**aith of our fathers, holy faith.* On the overhead projector the words scrolled down. *We will be true to thee till death.* And then the principal, a veteran who'd lost three fingers in the Second World War, began The Lord's Prayer. Summer was over and four hundred kids bowed their heads in mourning. Not Allie though. She was nudging my ribs and pointing to the group of middle-aged women off to one side of the stage. Long pleated skirts, orthopaedic shoes, hair in crimped waves.

"Look," she whispered. "There."

I stood on my toes. The principal droned on. Announcements and news and rules, rules, rules. And then he was saying, "Two new members will be joining our staff," he was saying, "Fresh out of university," saying, "Let's welcome Miss Luke and Mr. Dickinson." A slim blonde woman stepped out from behind the curtain and kids hooted and stamped their feet but when a man in a brown sports jacket and thin necktie appeared beside her the auditorium exploded. Beneath the stage lights, they looked like a little marzipan couple on a wedding cake.

"Holy cripes," Allie said, "get a load of him."

*

MR. DICKINSON WAS a dreamboat, a living doll, all the Beatles rolled into one. Allie and I couldn't take our eyes off him. We shifted in our desks, heads swivelling as he strolled up and down the aisles, throwing a piece of chalk in the air, catching it on the way down. We watched him shrug off his jacket and loosen his tie. As he rolled up his shirt sleeves, exposing his forearms. His eyes were deep set, his jaw strong. And his pockmarked skin? In our opinion it only made him more ruggedly handsome. We watched him rub his jaw and fiddle with his watch strap, slipping it around his wrist. And the dark hairs on that wrist. The damp patches beneath his arms when he reached up with the ten-foot pole to open a top window. Every move he made. Every object he touched.

The wooden pointer!

He dragged its rubber tip through a canyon's deep chasm. "Erosion," he said, "wind and water, the timeless wearing away." Here an isthmus, there a peninsula. He directed our gaze toward a distant headland, a mesa's abrupt rise. What we discovered that September:

1. Land forms were various and beautiful.
2. We had a sudden longing for beauty.
3. There weren't enough hours in a day to satisfy our longing.

While the rest of the sixth grade took out their coloured pencils and filled in their maps, Allie and I stole glances at the man looking out the window, hands in his pockets, sucking on a eucalyptus drop. We watched with a single-minded intensity, afraid he might sail over the horizon and disappear.

*

BY THE SECOND WEEK, Miss Luke's third grade students so adored her they swarmed her whenever she stepped out for recess duty. Little kids fought viciously to hold one of her hands. Mr. Dickinson liked her too. One morning they stood by her car talking so long they were both late for first buzzer. At lunch Allie and I went to the parking lot to search for clues. We circled Mr. Dickinson's car, kicking its tires, like salesmen or potential buyers. We checked the doors and speedometer; we peered into the back seat. An empty packet of Export A, a pair of shoes without laces, a couple of library books: *My Family and Other Animals, An Innovative Approach to the Modern Classroom.* Dangling from Miss Luke's rear view mirror was a little white poodle with a tag that said *Fee Fee*.

A few days later, playing basketball after school, we looked across the asphalt. Miss Luke was entering the annex, wearing a turtleneck sweater and stretchy green stirrup pants.

"Now things are heating up," Allie said.

I took a shot. The ball rolled around the rim before falling through with a whoosh.

"Hubba hubba," she said. "Hubba hubba ding ding."

*

Mr. Dickinson handed out mimeographed lyrics of songs. No more *Sur le Pont d'Avignon*? No more *Michael Row the Boat Ashore*? The windows were open and Indian summer hung in the air, limpid as fruit. He took a guitar from its case and started to play. My favourites: *If I had a Hammer, Where have all the Flowers Gone*. Allie liked *The Ballad of Tom Dooley*, a woman murdered for love, a dead man swinging from an oak tree.

We'd never heard anything as thrilling as the sound of our own voices.

After school we hung around Mr. Dickinson's desk. Could we clean the boards? Sharpen his pencils? He looked up and smiled. "I appreciate you asking, girls, but, really, I can manage."

We begged for a detention. Confessed to passing notes, abusing washroom privileges.

"Vamoose," he said, and when we didn't, he said it again.

We still didn't move so he got up and walked around his desk, bringing with him cigarette smoke, aftershave, exotic male sweat.

"I'm not asking again."

Outside the classroom, Allie dropped to her knees, hands pressed together in prayer. "You don't mean it," she said to the closed door. "Say you don't mean it."

"Oh, Allie," I said. "Get up."

*

The afternoon of Open House, my mother was too preoccupied with my younger sisters, one still in diapers, the other a toddler tugging against her leather harness, to do more than nod in my direction, then head out the door. I thought Allie's mum wasn't going to make it, but at 2:50 she appeared in the doorway in a corduroy mini skirt and white go-go boots, out of breath, beaming like someone who'd arrived late to a party. Her thick dark hair, parted at the side, sort of covered one eye and flipped up at the shoulders in a way I greatly admired. While Mr. Dickinson wrote next week's spelling words on the board, all the kids watched Allie's mum waving at Allie and me, a flutter of pink fingernails.

Allie slid down in her seat, trying to make herself invisible.

Her mum was the only divorcee I knew, the only mum with not one but two jobs — evening janitor and Avon Lady — but later that night she was home, making her gourmet macaroni casserole with pieces of fried sausage, stewed tomatoes, a crushed Cornflake topping. Her boyfriend, Mike, the latest in a string of policemen, was coming for dinner.

"Like him?" I said.

"Like who?" Allie's mum said.

"She knows who,"Allie said.

"*She* is the cat's mother," her mum said.

Allie was yanking tiny hairs off her kneecaps with eyebrow tweezers. Her mum dipped a finger into the cheese sauce, and then licked. She closed her eyes.

"Yum," she said, and went back to stirring.

"Mr. Dickinson," I said.

She made a kissing noise and I giggled.

"Mum!" Allie said.

"Well, honey, he's cute," she said, defensively. "Why blame me for the way things are?"

"You didn't have to do that."

"Do what?"

"You could just say he's nice."

"She's just bugging you," I said to Allie.

"Oh, don't get your precious tail in a knot," her mum said.

At the sink, dumping macaroni into the colander, she puckered her lips and glanced at me slyly, and then the phone rang. It was Mike saying he couldn't make it.

I'd liked some of her boyfriends. Last summer one had taken Allie and me in his convertible to Qualicum Beach where he and her mum had slathered each other with coconut oil then lain side by side on a sleeping bag, holding hands for hours. But not Mike. I didn't like anything about him, not his high leather boots, the gun in his holster or his big square hands. Sometimes on his dinner break he'd roar up on his motorcycle and storm into the house without knocking or saying hi. He and Allie's mum would lock themselves in her bedroom and twenty minutes later he'd roar away.

She shoved the casserole in the oven: "Then it's just us three ladies tonight."

"Boo hoo," Allie said. "Don't make me cry."

*

WE WERE LEANING against the chain-link fence eating black plums when Mr. Dickinson and Miss Luke pushed through the swinging front doors of the main building. Allie wiped her hands on her skirt. "At last," she said, and spat out a pit.

Crossing the schoolyard, Miss Luke stepped around puddles, her long white fingers gesturing languorously as she talked. Mr. Dickinson strode alongside her, swinging his briefcase.

"She doesn't even walk like a normal person," Allie said. "Look, she tiptoes!"

We headed over to the bike racks and crouched down where we could get a good view of the parking lot without being seen. Sure enough, Miss Luke and Mr. Dickinson got into the same car. *Her* car of all things.

After that, Allie wanted to know their whereabouts at all times. In notepads we made charts and maps and graphs, noting their movements, how often they were seen together, what they were wearing. In the morning or afternoon? Alone or in other teachers' company? Did they talk in the parking lot before or after school? How long did they talk? Did they leave in separate cars or the same car? How often did she come down to the annex? On what pretext? On a scale of ten, how did he look? Zero was miserable. Ten was ecstatic.

*

Mr. Dickinson made the following announcement: from now on, one student would be chosen as boy or girl of the week. The classroom door would highlight the chosen student's work, along with his or her self-portrait, and for the duration of the week that student would be a sort of honoured guest.

"What's that?" Harvey Gibbs asked, and Mr. Dickinson said an honoured guest was someone you treated with special respect. Harvey, who sat a few seats ahead of me, let the boys use him as a punching bag. To the girls he talked ad nauseam about how he was going to protect the country from the Russian commies. He'd failed three years in a row.

The following Monday after assembly Allie and I raced into the annex and along with the rest of the class crowded around the door. Beneath the girl of the week banner was Sheila Battersall's name written in calligraphy. Below that: her perfect spelling test, her perfect arithmetic quiz, her Social Studies test on land forms with a blue star in the top left corner. She'd even identified the unidentifiable Oxbow Lake. In the centre of all this brilliance was Sheila's self-portrait, its adorable likeness, her pug nose and freckles, even her widow's peak.

A few weeks later, I was chosen, I was the one, me — Jean Marie Waterman — and my self-portrait and quizzes were pinned artfully to the door. Allie didn't say anything, she just went to her desk and pulled out the exercise book she wrote random thoughts in for the first ten minutes of each day. That week I floated around in a pleasant daze. Now I understood what it meant to be an honoured guest. It meant you felt like it was your birthday, five days running. A week later when it was Allie's turn, she still didn't say anything. Not to me, not to her mum, though I got the feeling she thought being "Girl of the Week" was some kind of secret between her and Mr. Dickinson.

And then her mum, writing up invoices at the kitchen table, said, "By the way, honey, I dropped into the annex today. Girl of the Week, wow, I'm proud of you."

Allie looked horrified. "Why'd you do that? The door thing's for me, not you."

"Well, sorr-ree, but your very nice teacher said he appreciates parents dropping by."

She picked up a pamphlet Mr. Dickinson must have given her and began to read: "*Parental involvement is an important building block in a child's academic success.*"

"I'm not listening to anything you say," Allie said.

"He said I could drop by any time to discuss your progress."

Allie's mum said progress as though it were a threat or a taunt, and Allie scowled murderously and turned up the volume on the radio, and I thought again how she and her mum didn't act like any daughter and mother I knew. The window was slightly ajar and a gust of wind blew the invoices off the table.

"In fact," her mum said, gathering up the bits of paper and clutching them to her chest, "he said he'd be happy to see me any time."

"I doubt that," Allie said. "I seriously doubt that very much."

*

ALLIE'S HAIR KEPT whipping across her eyes as she tried to take down Miss Luke and Mr. Dickinson's license numbers. Garbage cans rattled against their chains, candy wrappers hopped across the asphalt. She turned to me, eyes stinging with tears. "So what'd you get?"

I read from my note pad: "*November 18, 1964, 12:45 p.m., seen in staff room, reading.*"

"That's no good. *What* was he reading? The newspaper? A letter? His diary?"

"I don't want to do this any more," I said.

Allie's long, oriental blue eyes widened. "Fine, if that's the way you want to be, then fine."

"Don't be like that. I still think he's the best teacher ever, I just don't want to spy on him all the time."

"In case you're interested, *she's* doing the Girl of the Week thing in her class now."

"So?"

"*So?* So she's copying him."

And then the first Monday of December. Staring back at us from the classroom door: Harvey Gibbs' grinning self-portrait surrounded by his sloppy, corrected worksheets, a goofy-looking cadet's cap on his head.

Mr. Dickinson, we decided, had surely lost his way.

"And whose fault is it?" Allie said, her voice rising. "Miss Luke's, that's whose."

*

"HOLY MOLY," Allie whispered. Cutting through the schoolyard after dinner, we saw Mr. Dickinson and Miss Luke inside our brightly-lit annex classroom. She was smiling and tilting her head; he was frowning. Her hair, normally pulled back in a ponytail, was loose around her face. How flushed, I thought, how pretty.

"What does he see in her?" Allie said. "I mean, *what?*"

We watched in silence, as the night chill seeped through our sweaters, and then Allie began to chant softly to herself, "Shame shame on Mis-ter Dickinson, shame shame on Mis-ter Dickinson." The more she repeated the words the less they seemed to mean. They ran together, became senseless, a kid's song, and despite myself, I was drawn in and started to chant along with her. Our voices grew louder and louder until Mr. Dickinson walked across the room and looked out the window. I thought he shook his head before pulling down the blinds, all five of them, and I hoped he hadn't seen us. Allie seemed to panic, then, and began to shriek, "Shame, shame, shame!"

The following morning when I slipped into my desk, Mr. Dickinson, pacing in front of the board, wasn't throwing a piece of chalk into the air and catching it on the way down. He hadn't even switched on the overhead lights. There'd been a torrential downpour during the night and it was still spitting. The classroom smelled rank, of baloney sandwiches and wet boots. With his head down and his hands behind his back, he looked like a hunched monster in a fairy tale, not the man who'd strolled the aisles Friday afternoons, strumming his guitar and leading us in song.

I was afraid he would speak. Afraid he wouldn't. Kids were whispering, "What's going on?" Allie seemed unaware or indifferent, but I wondered why we'd done it. What had we wanted so badly? And now this awful figure striding back and forth, this waiting for him to turn and condemn us publicly for actions I couldn't explain even to myself. I wanted to stand and say, I swear it was only a joke, and then Harvey blurted out in his monotone voice, "Are we gonna sit here all day, Sir, because if we are can I go home?"

Mr. Dickinson cleared his throat. An incident had occurred the evening before, he began, an incident involving two individuals in the class. "The behaviour of these two individuals was" — and he paused to search for the appropriate word, a word that would convey the extent of his feelings — "disappointing."

The class expelled a sigh of relief. I looked at Allie. She rolled her eyes and Mr. Dickinson continued to talk about respect and boundaries and the right to privacy, and though he didn't look directly at Allie or me, I was sure everyone knew we were the guilty ones. I stared at the back of Harvey's big dumb head and for a moment I envied him. Right now, he was probably a thousand miles away, slumped on an ice floe somewhere in the Bering Strait, rifle aimed at the endless night.

"I'm not going to name names," Mr. Dickinson said, "but the two individuals to whom I am speaking know who they are."

*

WE SAT CROSS-LEGGED on the shag carpet, the Monopoly board between us, eating cottage cheese and ketchup sandwiches. Allie's hair was a smashed-down field of dark hay and there was a ripeness to her. She hadn't showered in days. The furnace roared up, then died down, roared up, died down. I bought hotels for Boardwalk and Park Place but Allie just sipped her Fanta. When I landed on Reading Railroad she continued to chew on her thumb and for the first time ever didn't snap her fingers and gloat. "Thank you very much, that'll be two hundred buckaroos."

The little balsam Christmas tree in the corner of the living room was decorated with strings of plain white popcorn. After a screaming match with her mum, Allie had removed all the baubles and tinsel because, Allie said, baubles and tinsel were tacky and tacky stuff made her physically sick.

Her mum was rushing around the house, getting ready for work. I pictured her at the law office downtown, swinging her hips while she vacuumed and emptied waste baskets, her little transistor attached to her belt loop. At the door, she zipped up her ski jacket with the faux fur collar and blew us kisses.

"Don't do anything I wouldn't do."

As soon as her car backed out of the driveway, Allie yelled "Raid!"

In her mum's bedroom she dumped the Avon suitcase upside down on the bed and we each grabbed a handful of lipstick samples. Standing in front of the vanity mirror, we tightened our lips across our teeth in hard cold smiles and studied our reflections. Allie was compact and shapely like her mum whereas I was long and stringy. I wanted to like the way I looked but I didn't. I liked the way Allie looked. That day my features looked so fractured and odd they didn't even seem to add up to a face.

We applied a colour to our lips then quickly wiped it off to apply another. *Cherries in the Snow, Coral Fusion, Sahara Red.* Kiss-imprinted tissues fell around our feet.

"I hate this," Allie said after a while. "I pretty much hate everything."

I suggested Beatle Boyfriends. She nodded. Beatle Boyfriends had been our favourite game the summer before; we'd had week-long marathons during which we'd spoken only in Liverpudlian accents. In the living room we pulled out the portable record player, then began to dance to "She Loves You." We shouted back and forth about whose turn it was to get which Beatle. That night I was resigned. She could have Paul if I got George *and* John.

"John's married," she shouted.

"Duh, I'm not an idiot."

"So how can he be your boyfriend?"

"We can *pretend* he's not married."

She held up her hands in a gesture of complete exasperation, and then twisted lower on the balls of her feet.

"What about Ringo?" I shouted. "You want him?"

"Fat chance."

"That's mean."

"*He's* mean."

"Ringo?"

"Mr. Dickinson," Allie said. "Hey, I've got a super idea. Say we invite him to the party but when he comes we ignore him and just dance with the Beatles."

*

WHO KNOWS WHY I agreed to go out with her that night looking for his house. As usual we piled on three sweaters each — making it through winter without wearing a coat was a matter of pride — but when we stepped outside it was strangely mild. Balmy even. Fog hung over the street. The air was so wet, it felt like you could reach out and squeeze it like a sponge. We started in the direction of Partridge Street, Allie saying, "If we just knew more about him. Something, anything."

At the corner store a car pulled up beside us and a boy stuck his head out the window. We stared ahead and walked as fast as we could without breaking into a run. The car rolled slowly alongside. Out the corner of my eye I could see the driver slouched down low, his eyes barely reaching the dash. And then the car lurched forward and screeched off, the boy at the window yelling, "Stupid bitches, stupid fucking little bitches."

We bolted into the park, past the swings and monkey bars, past the red dragon, its magnificent iron head. Beyond was Bowker's Bridge; beneath it a decomposing rat. Knowing this, we held hands and flew across the wooden planks. On Partridge Street we slowed and caught our breath, then began scouting up and down until we found number 35, a small yellow bungalow set back from the road on a narrow lot, a red Valiant parked in the driveway.

"So we know where he lives," I said. "Let's go."

But Allie wanted to play Knock Knock Ginger.

"You first," she said.

"This wasn't even my idea," I said.

"Just one puny little knock," she whined. "Then I'll do it."

"What if he's right there?"

"Say you thought your aunt lived here. You made a mistake."

I shook my head.

"Say you were selling Brownie cookies but ran out and now you're taking orders."

Allie wouldn't back down. I knew this. We'd been best friends for three years and I knew for a fact that backing down was not her way.

"Besides," she said, her bottom lip going soft and trembly, "he likes you better."

"He does not."

Allie's chin sort of quivered as she looked at the house and I knew she was trying to dredge up some tears.

"Okay," I said. "For Pete's sake, okay."

"Great," she said. "I'll wait there." She pointed to a laurel bush to the right of the steps.

For a few minutes, I stood on the welcome mat, staring at the doorknob which, bizarrely, was in the middle of the door. I reached out to touch it and the door slipped open and then I was looking straight into a dark room. The house was silent — at least he wasn't home — so I kept standing there, wondering what to do next.

"See anything?" Allie whispered.

I waited for my eyes to adjust and then I saw Mr. Dickinson's jacket thrown over a chair.

I turned. "His jacket."

"His jacket!" she squealed. "Go touch it."

I'd come that far. Why not touch his jacket, the soft wool and silk lining, the suede patches at the elbows? I stepped over the threshold into a room not unlike a beach cabin my family had once stayed in — the kitchen in the corner, stove and fridge and sink against the far wall. Above the table, a bare light bulb swung slightly at the end of a long cord. On the table was a bottle of milk. A blanket covered the couch and a few books and magazines were scattered on the rug. The whole thing looked eerily like a stage set, waiting for people to walk on and start speaking their lines. And then I saw, propped against the wall like an old friend, Mr. Dickinson's guitar, and I had the sudden urge to flee.

I took a breath and forced myself to walk across the room. I reached for the jacket and a box of eucalyptus drops rattled like something alive, and I dropped the jacket back on the chair. As I turned to go I heard little splashing sounds. Hushed murmurings. Human voices. Curious, and strangely fearless now, I walked over to the doorway I assumed led to other rooms, and then I was standing in a narrow hall that opened into a bedroom to my left and a bathroom to my right. The bathroom door was slightly ajar. I took a step toward it and with a jolt realized I was looking at two people in a bathtub. It was dark and the people hadn't noticed me, but now I was too terrified to move. Light from the street shone through the bathroom window, and I could see the shape of the woman's head, sleek as a seal's. I felt the drag of my sweaters, the outer sleeves hanging to my knees. The woman looked up and my brain shut down like a TV screen, a pinprick of light glowing in the centre. I think she spoke, then, but it's possible I just imagined her speaking.

Jean? she whispered. *Jean, is that you?*

The Eau de Parfum — Topaz, Sweet Honesty, Goddess, Peony — I'd sprayed on my neck earlier oozed from my pores. I stunk. I took a few steps backwards and when neither Allie's mum nor Mr. Dickinson objected, I turned the corner into the big room and headed straight for the door. As I closed it behind me, I thought I heard him say, "Did you just see what I saw?"

I leapt down the stairs and grabbed Allie's arm. "Let's get out of here."

"Were they smooching?"

"Come on, let's go."

"But you saw her?"

"I'll tell you later."

Allie was the fastest sprinter in sixth grade but that night I tore ahead, wanting to get as far as possible from the yellow bungalow and the people inside it.

"What were they doing, then?" Allie called. "Wait up. If they weren't smooching, what were they doing?"

At the park I cut diagonally across the marshy field, unbuttoning my top cardigan, pulling my arms out of the sleeves.

"I had a feeling she'd be there," Allie said, breathing heavily, a few steps behind. "I just had this feeling."

And then we were side by side, not talking anymore, just running and jumping over gullies and ditches, and after what seemed like years we were walking down the middle of our street, gasping and heaving, our runners covered in mud, our pants soaked through to the skin.

"Didn't I tell you?" Allie said when she could speak. "Right from the beginning, didn't I say he was hot for Miss Luke?"

Miss Luke?

I closed my eyes and remembered how in that brief moment before I'd been discovered, Mr. Dickinson had kissed Allie's mum's neck, making her whimper, a helpless shuddering whimper that could have meant anything. I thought of Mr. Dickinson strolling the aisles, singing "Hang down your head Tom Dooley," Allie belting out the harmony as though her heart would break.

She started to laugh. She laughed and laughed and then she was laughing so hard she had to sit on the curb and cross her legs.

"You saw," she said, "you saw everything."

I yanked the third sweater up over my head, the last scalding skin, and then dropped the bundle of soggy wool onto her lap. I sat beside her and right away my knees went spastic. The fog seemed to be rising from the pavement, swallowing us up, but I could still see Allie's face, triumphant in the smudged light of the street lamp, and I knew I'd never tell her. Not then, not ever.

"Stop that," she said, slapping my legs.

I clamped my hands over my knees but they kept knocking together as though they belonged to something mechanical and broken.

"I said stop."

I fell forward, wrapped my arms around my thighs and held on. "I can't," I said. "They won't."

SEATTLE

From the wings of the stage two men appear. Ushers? Reveen's bodyguards? I'm singing as they come toward me. I'm doing something interesting with my hips. The men are wearing maroon uniforms, piping down the sides of their pant legs.

"Hey, what is this?"

Hands cup my elbows. They lift me up, sweep me away.

"Looks like your grand finale, lady."

My face is wet. Tears? Impossible. Tears?

*

THIS FRAGILE EMOTIONAL state began around the time I accepted Lana's dinner invitation. I'm not comfortable watching strangers put food into their mouths. Adam says my attitude is the result of the unwholesome environment in which I was raised. He says I reject nourishment in any form. I'm dealing with my stuff, I tell him. It's the same for everyone.

Normally, I'd have invented an implausible excuse. Life is implausible. Last week, a stabbing at a Tupperware party, police and brawling women, hysterical budgies, blood-speckled walls.

I went to my cousin's dinner party because she invited me, and because I was curious, and because Adam didn't want to go, and because I was in that kind of a mood.

I had my reasons.

Lana sits on the board of several artistic enterprises, and writes movie and book reviews — skewers, all of them — and she's always being interviewed on CBC about some cultural phenomenon or another. Everyone wants Lana Buchanan's opinion. Most of the time she looks wildly exasperated. As my mother says, Lana never did suffer fools.

The night of the dinner party she glows and why not? She's the curator of a trendy art gallery, drives a custom-built Volkswagen Bug. She's got a new man *and* a new house. The walls on the main floor have been painted three times; she's still not sure they're the right shade of taupe. She's wearing taupe too — pants, turtleneck shell, sling-back sandals. It's hard to believe that a year earlier she washed up on my doorstep, a human wreck. Since then, and without either of us saying a word, it's understood: that was then, this is now.

"See," Lana says, leaning over my shoulder, "the property retreats to the point of a triangle." The backyard is a riot of native plants, green dissolving into black. Sword ferns, Oregon grape, salal. Lana likes things to appear natural; she likes to give the impression she's not trying too hard.

∗

Georgia: climbing over me, my loose-limbed fragrant girl. "Mmm, baby," I say, inhaling the calamine lotion I rubbed on her skin earlier. The toilet seat drops and then the sound of pee hitting the water. Wrapped in a quilt, Adam draws himself up on his side of the bed, like he's warding off some kind of threat. When Georgia doesn't come back I get up and walk down the hall to the kitchen. She's standing on a chair pushed against the counter. I switch on the light and she cries and covers her face with her hands. All the cupboards are open. Soup mix, wheat germ, coffee beans spilled over the counter. Her pyjama top is on the floor. Also a carton of milk tipped on its side: shimmering white pool.

"Baby," I say, "it's three in the morning."

Georgia smiles a vacant smile and I'm looking down the tunnel of my own childhood.

"I'm making brownies for you and Daddy."

She goes back to stirring the empty metal bowl with a wooden spoon, and I bend to kiss the small of her back. She dumps a tin of cocoa into the bowl. A puff of brown smoke billows around us. I pick her up, spoon and all, and carry her back to our bed, thinking, It's the texture of things that repulses me. Eggs, butter, the stink of animal fat.

Georgia sleepwalks. Every few nights I wake up to find her.

∗

REVEEN'S SATIN VEST is pink, nail polish pink, the colour of a 1957 convertible or a deadly jungle flower. Pam's jogging suit is the softest pink imaginable. Lying on the floor, she kicks her feet in the air like a gigantic newborn.

∗

WE GO OUR separate ways: I stop for a bottle of wine to bring to Lana's dinner party and Adam and Georgia drive out to the summerhouse. It's one of those dreary spring evenings that asks nothing of you, just that you keep your head above water. I imagine Georgia and Adam sitting on the point, dampness seeping through their jeans. A little sailboat anchored in the cove. Bagpipes droning. I remember sitting on that very spot when Lana and I were kids, her saying Finlayson Arm, the land across the water, was actually Russia. If we got up early, we could paddle over the next day. Was I up for it?

Of course I was. I was up for anything Lana suggested. Tomorrow we'd lie belly-down on air mattresses, paddle to Vladivostock.

Our grandfather bought the summerhouse in the sixties when waterfront was going for a song. Hameldaeme, he called it, meaning: Home Will Do Me. Since then, Lana's and my father, the Buchanan brothers, have taken a perverse pride in altering nothing. The summerhouse is a kind of museum right down to the faded wallpaper, cracked linoleum and wall plaques with bleak Scottish proverbs written on them: *Be happy while you're living, for you're a long time dead.* Above the fireplace there's a moth-eaten flag, the cross of St. Andrew. Two identical armchairs are shoved up against the wall, like a disgruntled old couple.

Lana and I are in our teens, sitting in those chairs, which we've dragged onto the porch. It's late, our parents have gone to bed, a neighbour's cat is clawing one of the chair's upholstery to green fuzz. Lana's arguing because she's good at it and I'm arguing because I don't have a choice. That night I say Hameldaeme is alive. She says it isn't. I say it is, and why does she have to be so damn definite about everything?

"Buildings are inanimate," she says.

"But this one isn't. Sometimes I can hear it talking."

"If I were you, I'd keep that to myself."

But I know what I know. When we leave in September, the walls will pick up where they left off; they'll resume their decades-old conversation, revert to their strange, musty, organic selves.

"Shh," I say. "Listen."

∗

LANA'S HOUSE is across from the Chinese cemetery. It's famous for the huge iron bell stolen from a temple during the Boxer Rebellion and then smuggled into Canada. I ring and Levi answers. He bows slightly from the waist.

"Hello. You must be . . ."

Black hair, deep-set blue eyes. Great looking, despite the scar. Lana's mentioned the accident, that he's needlessly self-conscious. Do I just imagine a look of relief on his face? Relief that I'm a flake and nothing like Lana?

The other guests arrive, two women, both artists, both divorced, and Roland, Lana's assistant. He flops down on the leather couch and arches an eyebrow. Lana says she invites Roland to all her dinner parties because he makes the furniture look fabulous.

She walks around the room with a tray of martinis, talking about her real estate agent who, apparently, told her the house was a great deal if she didn't mind the neighbours. Lana makes a ghostly hoot and Levi offers to take me and my martini on a tour of the renovations. Upstairs, we look around, admiring.

"All Lana, all the time." he says. "She's a talented lady."

In the bathroom I get into the Jacuzzi tub and slide down. "I love vermouth," I say. "There are few things in life as good as vermouth."

Levi agrees that Lana mixes a wicked martini.

She's had walls removed, skylights and windows put in to take advantage of the views: the Olympic Mountains and Juan de Fuca Strait. She's that kind of person — always taking advantage. I don't mean that negatively. She can't help the way she is. Even she doesn't know what's

42

driving her. Once when I asked, Lana said, "I don't understand your question, Char. What do you mean, *drive*?"

I like drinking on an empty stomach. You lose yourself quickly. The edges blur before you've had time to say, "My granddaddy was born on Loch Rannoch." If Adam were here he'd insist I eat something — crackers, a piece of bread. We'd argue. I'd accuse him of mothering me and he'd say I was acting like a spoiled brat. But he's at Hameldaeme with Georgia. Right now they're probably playing the Rocky Horror album on the old console, Georgia whooping it up, singing *Let's do the time warp*. Tomorrow morning, Adam will make pancakes with blueberries that Georgia will meticulously pick out. The first time he suggested they give me a night to myself, I welcomed the break, but more and more I suspect their nights at the cove are a break from me.

The smell of baking chicken wafts up Lana's staircase. I feel light-headed, nauseous. Fact: there is more lethal bacteria on the skin of your average factory-farmed chicken than in the water of your average toilet bowl. I tell Levi I read that somewhere. Useless details like this stick to the inside of my head.

"Watch your step." He holds out a hand. A real gentleman.

Lana's been married twice, not to mention the countless lovers. Cavalier doesn't come close to describing her attitude toward men. After dumping her second husband — a British antique dealer who, incredibly, wore a tweed jacket and carried a big black umbrella — Lana threw a women-only party. After making a toast to the joys of single life, she announced that at long last women had made men redundant. "And you know what happens to redundant tissue, don't you? It turns malignant."

"That's so unfair," I say.

"I'm just quoting Germaine Greer."

If you believe Lana, both her ex-husbands are self-centred jerks. The first, now the conductor of an orchestra in Boston, is living with a model fifteen years younger than himself. At least that's what Lana says. I've heard differently. The woman *was* a model. Now she's a speech therapist teaching young children where to place their wayward tongues.

*

REVEEN INVITES one of the volunteers to the front of the stage. Pam, overweight, with bad posture, sort of grovels toward him, clearly enthralled to be assistant, puppet, whatever he asks of her. Her doe eyes and milkmaid complexion make me think of the Spanish Armada. Not the actual warships, but the words Spanish and Armada.

Reveen takes one of Pam's hands and raises it in the air like she's a prize fighter. "Ladies and gentlemen, Miss A-mer-i-ca."

As though startled from sleep, she's suddenly erect, throwing back her shoulders, thrusting her breasts forward. The tip of her chin lifts sweetly into the air as Reveen places a doll-sized bouquet in her arms. She plants a kiss on his cheek, and then walks across the stage, waving to the crowd. Before our eyes she's transformed into someone born to the spotlight. She's poised and ageless, everyone's long lost friend. I glance at the faces of my fellow volunteers. They're all thinking the same thing: Where has Pam been all these years? How we have missed her. The theatre falls silent. Is she beautiful? If not, then something else. Something indescribably lovely.

*

LANA HAS a way about her. The clouds part. They parted wide that summer afternoon.

We're eleven and thirteen, waiting in line at the Crystal Pool for one last dive. Shivering. My head aches from the chlorine and bathing cap. The lifeguard walks by, wearing the same revealing trunks he's worn every other day of summer. Lana swivels her head. Smiles. Bull's eye. Shot through the heart. I swear he staggers.

"Sexy," Lana says, as though sexy is an immeasurable truth I will never understand.

We crouch in the shallow end, submerged to our necks, the lifeguard blowing his whistle. And then longer, more shrilly. In the change room, we're shaky with hunger, but realize we've spent all our money. Lana insists we go to the cafe anyway.

"Ask someone for change," she says.

"Ask who?"

"Anyone. That woman with the kid. Him."

Sitting on a wicker chair tucked beneath a palm tree, a man in a long cardigan and plastic thongs is drinking a glass of pale tea. His toenails are yellow claws.

"Ask him yourself," I say.

"You're the one with spunk."

"Spunk?"

"Everyone says so."

"Who says?"

"Your dad, mine. They say it all the time. That Char, she sure has spunk."

"You're older."

"It's different for me. Can't you see the difference?"

I wait for what's coming, and then Lana says, half joking, that she's got her dignity to think of.

My dignity too, I think, but we both know.

"Go," she says. "I'm dying here."

I walk around the cafe, in a kind of daze, no longer hungry, asking and receiving, a quarter here, a nickel there. I'm only a little surprised that it's actually working and soon I've got enough for two plates of chips.

Walking home, I sort of dawdle behind Lana, past the totem pole museum and Haida carvers, their forearms etched with scars. I dawdle past the petting zoo, the llamas and potbellied pigs, around the wood-chip path, the baseball field, and when we're near her street, she stops and turns. "You can walk beside me now."

Those last moments, floating on my back, hair loose, looking up through the glass ceiling, the panorama of smouldering sky. The pool empty of everyone, even Lana.

*

Lana and her friends seem to cluster at one end of the table, leaving Levi and me at the other end. He's talking about Woody Allen's latest movie, that it's bigger, more austere, witty but not funny. There's a difference. Lana and her friends are gossiping about a woman neither Levi nor I know: Marne Solaris, an Art History professor who can't go two minutes without calling someone a lousy motherfucker. Apparently, she's fallen in love with an electrician from Esquimalt.

"Esquimalt," Roland says. "Oh, Lana, say it's not so."

I don't like academics. Or maybe I don't like academia. Or maybe it's the hothouse atmosphere inside the actual buildings I don't like. Adam teaches statistics in the Sociology Department. He's a sessional, who, like sessionals everywhere, wants a real job. There are thousands like him, overqualified and growing bitter as liverwort.

"I give them six months," Lana says. "No, five."

I'm not saying she's purposely excluding me, but she isn't making an effort to include me either. I pick at my rice, avoiding the chicken breast stuffed with pine nuts and prunes. Slime covered in grease!

Levi leans forward. "I envy you," he says quietly.

"Really? How so?"

He wishes he'd had a kid, he says. But never the right woman at the right time. "When you think about it, a child is the only person you can have a relationship with from the beginning of their life to the end of yours." But you never know. Maybe he and Lana.

I reach for the wine and pour myself a full glass. As granddad Buchanan used to say, "They talk about my drinking, but not about my thirst."

And now Lana's talking about Jeff, the guy Marne was married to for eighteen years, this totally fit guy who keeled over on the soccer field last year.

Roland says: "Good god, relationships aren't meant to last that long."

Lana's speaking in a voice I recognize — imperious but somehow cajoling too — which can mean only one thing: she's about to launch into a story and wants everyone's attention.

After the funeral Marne told Lana that Jeff had started leaving the house mysteriously in the evenings in the months before his stroke. Marne questions him but he's vague, then truculent. One night, after a couple of vodkas, she gets in her car and follows at a distance, ending up at the Empress in the Tourist Only parking lot.

"Tourist only?" Roland says. "Who says who's a tourist? I mean, huh?"

"So there's Marne," Lana continues, "crouching in the rose garden, watching Jeff cross Government Street. You know, where the double-decker buses line up."

She pauses. Radiant smile. Everyone following?

Jeff seems to know a tour guide; one of those pretty university girls who sells tickets flouncing around in a short skirt.

Roland rolls his eyes: "Pretty can be so lame."

The artists nod.

I've always hated Lana's stories. No, I hate the way she tells them, monopolizing the conversation and forcing everyone to listen. I glance at Levi who's watching Lana, a dopey look on his face. His skin is clean, almost velvety. I want to touch his scar.

Jeff talks to the tour guide for about ten minutes, then walks back to his car and drives home. Marne follows him the next night and the one after that, always a little drunk, and it's always the same thing. Straight to the Empress and across the street to the tour guide. Talking to this girl appears to be the extent of it, but Marne can't help herself. All through August she follows him, crouching in the rose garden with binoculars. And then one night, after Labour Day, Jeff stays put. That's the end of it.

Around the table, there's a few moments of silence — everyone trying to understand the point of Lana's story — and then the woman to my left says, "That Jeff guy must have been one lousy motherfucker."

The other woman laughs in a tight hiccuppy way and Lana looks down the length of the table at me as though I'm a stranger who's just walked in and she's not sure whether to welcome me or call the cops, and I think, I've got nothing against her. Not especially. After all, she's my cousin. She's got great clothes. She's got terrific hair. What's there not to like?

"Char," she says, "you're looking sort of tragic."

"Tragic's stylish," I say, "like taupe."

She turns back to her audience: "Marne doesn't question Jeff and he doesn't offer an explanation. They just go on as though nothing has happened. And then he buys it, just like that, chasing down a ball."

47

Roland shrugs. The women too. Lana seems sort of pensive and pissed off by their reaction. Levi jumps up and opens another bottle of wine on the sideboard, and then walks around the table replenishing glasses while the artists move on to *Pink!*, the latest art installation at Exchanges. They discuss the notion of cross-cultural colour terminology, pink's feminist, antifeminist, post-feminist connotations. They muse on its seminal place in nature.

Roland says, "The nipple, the nipple, the nipple."

"Georgia loves pink," I say. "Everything, and I mean everything I buy her has to be pink. But I think it's sort of infantalizing. Like panties."

Everyone's staring at me. Lana looks particularly alarmed. How drunk am I?

"Not the underwear," I say, calmly, enunciating. "Panties is a creepy word."

Levi says, "Are you all right, Char?"

I raise my empty glass to my lips. Christ, how would I know? After three hours in the company of Lana's friends how would I know anything? With the tip of my tongue I slurp up the last drop and then rise to me feet.

"You will have to excuse me," I say. "I am going to phone a cab."

*

LANA: ALWAYS THERE, always ahead, just fifteen months, but brighter, fiercer, stronger. Long-distance runner limping into the schoolyard, telling the track coach she doesn't mind the pain. Her ambition exhausts me; it makes me sad. And then the night she arrived at the door, wearing the poncho she'd bought in San Francisco. Hair wet around her face. No make-up, just a little lip gloss. I hadn't seen her in months. Whenever I'd phoned she was rushing to catch a plane or off to an opening. I led her into the living room where Georgia was sitting cross-legged on a pile of couch cushions. Lana rarely noticed Georgia except to observe that she controlled my life, but now she looked at Georgia with an addled expression.

"Hey, kiddo," she said.

"This is Pumpernickel Island," Georgia said.

"Got a boat?" Lana asked.

Georgia pulled up her feet, tucking them under her bum, and looked suspiciously down at the carpet. "Sharks," she said. Lana ran a finger across Georgia's cheek.

"Lana's crying," Georgia said.

I called Adam from his study, and after he'd persuaded Georgia to go to her room for a story, Lana sat on the floor in front of the gas fireplace and I sat on the hassock beside her. She began to talk about the affair she'd been having with a married man, a man she loved, the only man she'd really loved, the man she imagined spending her life with. It couldn't go on, he'd told her. Three kids, a wife with chronic fatigue. Lately the sight of his face in the mirror sickened him.

Lana pulled a Kleenex from her pocket, blew her nose, and then reached over to touch the tulips on the side table, their frilly two-toned edges.

"Mutants," she said distractedly. "Must be some kind of mutants."

"I had no idea," I said.

"It's over," she said, "I can't believe it's over. It's like a death, Char. It's worse than a death. I feel a thousand years old."

"You're only thirty-eight."

"Oh god," she moaned, "that is so old to be alone."

I heard Adam chase Georgia down the hall and into the bathroom, and then the bath water running. Lana looked up at me, her face drawn with pain, pain so pure and luminous it was almost a gift. And then she gripped my upper arms as though I were a life raft and she were drowning. Gently, I tried to extract her nails, but they dug deeper into my skin. If she were going down, she was determined to take me with her.

*

It's after twelve when I fall into bed, fully clothed. The kids in the next yard are still jumping on their trampoline beneath night lamps. Georgia likes to stand at the window watching them bounce above the fence. Head, no head. Head, no head.

On Lana's front steps, Levi and I stood for a moment listening to teenagers throw rocks at the cemetery bell. I looked into his eyes, the bottomless eyes of someone who's been swimming against the current for too long, and said, "Lana hates kids. She doesn't want one. Not with you, not with anyone. I'm just telling you this because you're a nice man, but you're a stand-in, Levi, you're the latest sucker."

With every clang, I heard, "Doom, doom, doom."

Those were Adam's brother's words when we told him we were getting married. Georgia was six months old.

"A hex," I said at the time. "People don't realize the power."

The branches of the maple chafe against the side of the house, the windows rattle in their casements, and I remember a breathless afternoon out at the cove, the flat calm water. Adam and I were eating roasted almonds on the wharf when I told him I finally understood why it's called making love.

"Every time we make love it *makes* me love you."

"So that's how it works," he said.

I flicked an almond at his chest. "Sex makes me love you, it makes you love me. It's not about choice. Our bodies make love happen."

For the first time in my life I felt utterly helpless and absolutely safe. The very idea of breaking up seemed incomprehensible, something that happened on other planets, to different species.

"If you want to know why people break up," Adam said, "ask Lana."

In the lobby of the Yarrow Building, the morning of our wedding, we almost did break up.

"No one does that anymore," he said when I informed him that I wanted to take his name. "It's outdated. Patriarchal."

"But we're a family. You, me, Georgia."

"You're a Buchanan. That's who you are."

*

Bruce Cockburn, the Winnipeg Ballet, a private screening of Michael Moore's *Bowling for Columbine*. Lana gets comps to events around town. She gives away the scraps. Most recently: Reveen, World Famous Hypnotist.

Adam says, "Let's go."

"You have *got* to be kidding. Why can't she give us tickets to something we might actually enjoy?"

"Hang on. This has nothing to do with Lana. Remember me? I'm talking here."

"When Brubeck came. She knows we love Brubeck but do you think!"

"I've always wanted to see one of these guys, ever since I was a kid."

On Thursday night I'm in a foul mood when we drop Georgia at my mother's and then drive to the Royal Theatre. Adam attempts conversation; he even whistles and cracks jokes. The whole Reveen thing has set my teeth on edge, but the truth is I get this way for no reason. Even if I wanted to, I couldn't dig myself out.

"Buck up," Adam says. "I hear it's good clean family entertainment."

He can be so goddamned superior, I think as he pulls into the parking lot and turns off the engine. Hands on the steering wheel, still looking ahead, he says, "There's something you need to know."

"Shoot," I say.

He clenches his jaw and then blurts out something about the night I went to Lana's dinner party, how he took Georgia to a friend's for a sleep-over, how they didn't go to Hameldaeme after all.

"I'm not following," I say.

"I flew down to Seattle."

Still, nothing computes. Seattle? Rainy city on Puget Sound, great bookstores, maritime museum, Space Needle, revolving restaurant? And then I remember: last spring, the flurry of academic conferences. Adam's delayed flight, his missed connections.

You don't sleep with someone for seven years and not know what you know.

I follow him dumbly into the empty lobby as the orchestra swells to a pitch. A cymbal crashes. We find our seats — a few rows from the front, dead centre — just as Reveen is finishing his spiel. I glance over at Adam, leaning forward, pushing his glasses up on his nose. Seattle or no Seattle, he's into this big time.

"Explore the farthest reaches of your mind," Reveen says, and a drum rolls. And then he's asking for volunteers. Hands fly up, a few people are rising, walking toward the stage. The next thing I know I'm wriggling past the row of knees. "Excuse me. Excuse me." I walk up the aisle and sit in a semicircle with the other volunteers beneath a bank of blinding lights. We all look out at the crowd, blinking, seeing nothing.

Reveen struts back and forth, a puffed-up bird, making chirping noises. We, the volunteers, have nothing to fear, he says. *We* are in control. We hold the strings. It's about focusing, it's about the unconscious and the power of suggestion, and then he goes on to suggest: our shoes are ringing telephones (the man beside me yanks off his boot, holds it to his ear); gold coins are falling out of our noses (a few people stick fingers up their nostrils); we're infants (a dumpy middle-aged woman in a pink jogging suit rolls on the floor, cooing and babbling); we've lost our navels (a miniature but perfectly proportioned East Indian man crawls on hands and knees, searching); a tiger's loose (a woman stands on her chair and cowers).

I watch through a sheer and billowy curtain, dread and anticipation beading my skin, thinking, con job. Rigged. All plants. And then Reveen's voice is in my ear, thick as chocolate pudding. I rub my palms up and down my thighs. The way my jeans fit tonight, skin over skin. Later I'll remember fragments of things — energy of the cosmos, life force, a river of light — but right now I'm watching him turn to the audience.

"Please give a big hand to Shania Twain."

A cool wind blows across the stage. My spine's so taut you could pluck it like a harp string. I hike up my blouse, exposing my famous midriff, ease my jeans down over my hips and begin to gyrate. The audience roars. Reveen tosses me a cucumber, vacuumed-packed in cellophane. The phrase, *gird your loins,* passes through my mind, which, I'm certain, is an important message from my unconscious. I hold the cucumber in both hands and lyrics pour from my mouth. My ribcage expands. People in the front row are standing and clapping.

What is Reveen doing? Why is he trying to take away my mike? I turn and hop away from him, odd little hopping motions, like Georgia's when she's pretending to be the frog in *Freddy the Freaky Frog.*

Reveen's clipped steps follow me across the stage. He snaps his fingers in my face. His insouciant grin.

"Back off, dude," I say.

He lays a hand on my shoulder.

I swat at him. "Just back right off."

I turn to the audience and open my arms. I am a wick dipped in oil. Heat enters my toes and spreads up through my ankles, calves, thighs, torso, chest, neck. My head bursts into flame. Somewhere out there in the sea of swaying bodies Adam is watching me burn.

UP THE CLYDE ON A BIKE

Before Dad left I talked about nothing except how much I wanted a horse. I said how miserable my life was and would continue to be without a horse of my own. The sixties were boom years and Dad, a welder, started going away every few weeks to work on construction. The first time he went Mum accused him of taking the job to get away from her.

"You think I'm bammy," she said.

"Don't talk that way," he said. "Say things like that you'll have me as daft as you."

They were sitting at the table and I was cantering around on Gondola, my imaginary horse. Between them an ashtray, the white porcelain swan with the thin curved neck.

"The money's too good to pass up," Dad said. "They're saying overtime. Double, triple pay." If he took advantage of all the work up island, he said, they could pay off the car, put a few bucks down on the mortgage. We could rent a beach cabin in Parksville next summer. Mum flicked ash into the swan's back and looked at him as though he'd just said we could rent a rocket and go to the moon. She stabbed her cigarette in the cavity between the outstretched wings and went to the broom closet. A door slammed and Mum returned with a mop. I stopped to watch her fill the sink with soap and water but Dad just ignored her and picked up the ashtray.

"Will you look at this," he said. "The poor wee birdie's lost an eye." On one side of the swan's head was a black bead; the other bead was missing. Mum started splashing the stringy mop over the linoleum. "Bloody hell, woman," Dad said. "Are you going to drown us out of house and home?"

Was he the crazy one? I wondered, wading out of the kitchen in wet socks. How could we rent a beach cabin? Had he forgotten that on her good days Mum didn't leave the house? On her bad days she didn't leave her bed?

*

BEFORE DAD LEFT Mum broke things — platters, ornaments, lamps. Dragging the vacuum down hallways and through rooms, she was a rampaging beast. Sometimes I'd sit on a stool in the kitchen watching her chop vegetables, imagining myself the calm centre of the world. Three whacks with the big knife and she'd drop chunks of cabbage into a boiling pot; water would spill over, extinguishing the gas flame. Mum would bring down the lid as though bringing down a cymbal.

Before Dad left my sister Sharon and I would walk to Quan Lee's Grocery after school, hating the metal cart because as far as we could tell only humpbacked old women pushed metal carts. Inside the store's entrance we'd take turns bouncing up and down on the mechanical horse, trying to coax life into its hard fixed saddle. At seven Sharon was small with thick glasses and ears that poked through her thin straight hair. Sometimes a man waiting for his wife at the checkout would take pity on Sharon and put a nickel in the metal box. For three minutes my sister would buck and holler *Atta girl, giddy up* with such wholehearted joy it was embarrassing to watch.

Before Dad left we were always forgetting things on Mum's shopping list. It might be steel wool or toilet paper or bobby pins. That day it was cigarettes. We watched her pull porridge oats and soup tins out of the bags. "Where's the fags? Jesus Christ, lassies, did I no give you money for fags?" While Mum searched for a pack of Matinee, I looked past her head at the tobacco tin, full of buttons, on top of the fridge. Wooden buttons, pearl buttons, glass buttons that rubbed against each other like flat shiny stones. The longer I stared at the tin the farther away it became. Blue speck at the wrong end of a telescope.

"You'll have to go back," Mum said finally. "That's all there is to it."

Sharon groaned. "Gloria can go."

"Why should I?" I said. "I always go."

Mum raised her tea to her mouth. "No fags," she said. "I'm fair disgusted with the pair of you."

Sharon picked up a bar of Ivory soap and inhaled. "Mmmm," she said. This was a diversionary tactic, and, I knew, useless. "Smells nice." Sharon sneezed and dropped the soap. She stuck her fingers in her ears and walked around the kitchen like a crazed rooster, head jerking, making clucking noises in her throat.

"I know what you two want." Mum looked from Sharon to me as though sizing us up, and then she drew in her breath and let it out slowly. "You want me in the nut house. Well, I'll be climbing the walls soon enough and then you'll see."

We'll see what?

By the time Dad came home from work we were exhausted, battle worn. We ate dinner in silence. Afterwards, he leaned back in his sleeveless undershirt and work pants, patting his stomach. "You're a right connoisseur of spuds, so you are," he said to Mum. "Now where's dessert?"

"Up my jumper," she said.

And they laughed. Every night the same dumb joke.

∗

Before Dad left, Sharon and I would climb the apple tree in the backyard, swinging down from a particular branch. We did this so many times, blisters formed on our palms. "Garden gloves," I said one afternoon, charging ahead of Sharon into the shed. Back in the tree, I reached for the branch but, without any grip, I slipped. When I came to, I was lying on the couch, Sharon was standing in the doorway holding an enormous leek, and Mum was shouting into the phone. "Can you no understand King's English? I said 4589 Blackwood Street." I glanced at my arm propped on a pillow. It was the shape of an S.

The taxi arrived and Mum said, "I'm awful sorry, hen. I cannee go with you."

"I know," I said, not knowing what I knew or why she could only stand on the top step, waving goodbye while the taxi driver carried me to the car. At the hospital I sailed down the hallway in a bed which slid through swinging doors into a room with blinding lights. A nurse placed something that looked like a toilet plunger over my mouth and said count backwards from ten.

Later that night Dad walked past my room and I wondered what he was doing in the children's ward of St. Joseph's Hospital. It didn't occur to me to call out and ask. He walked back and forth several times, finally coming into my room. His hair was combed back and he was wearing a sports jacket and tie. I'd never seen him look so handsome.

It had been a short fall but I'd broken two bones and cracked two more. The first doctor straightened the arm and set it in an L-shaped cast but after looking at an X-ray, the second doctor decided the first doctor had done a poor job. "Shoddy work," he said, rapping his knuckles on my plaster. The next day he broke and reset the bones.

The girl in the bed beside me talked non-stop about all the jello and ice-cream she was going to get after her tonsils came out. I'd never met such a jabber box. On the afternoon of her surgery, her mother sat on the edge of my bed, legs crossed at the ankles, waiting for her daughter to come out of the anaesthetic. She told me she'd once broken her own arm roller skating, and the only thing she could remember was that the skin inside her cast had been so itchy it had driven her crazy. I could feel her watching me as I tried to colour a picture of a zebra pushing an elephant on a swing. I was too old for colouring books but I was bored and needed to practice using my right hand. I planned on becoming fully ambidextrous before returning to school. And then the girl's mother asked if *my* mother would be visiting me that day.

"Probably tomorrow," I said.

After the surgery, the girl's face was bruised and swollen, and that night she lay facing the wall, sobbing. The next day she went home, a shadow of her former self, and I was alone in room 303, except for a baby who never cried. And then a nurse came and took the baby away and another nurse pushed the empty crib down the hall, one gimpy wheel hobbling to the elevator. I assumed the baby had died. Now I lived in dread of the nine o'clock juice cart because it meant the lights would go out and I'd lie awake for hours, heart pounding, waiting for death. I was convinced that one of these nights my bed would be removed as unceremoniously as the baby's crib.

*

BEFORE DAD LEFT he'd bring home news of the outside world — religious literature, women's magazines, political pamphlets handed out on street corners. One day he came home with a drugstore paperback: *Vinegar and Honey: Good Health the Natural Way.*

That spring Mum started to greet Dad at five o'clock with a tall glass of amber liquid. They'd sit on the back steps, smoking Matinees, and sipping slowly just as the author, a preacher from Minnesota, advised.

"Och," Dad would say, "bloody vile."

"Fair disgusting," Mum would answer.

Before Dad left my right eye twitched incessantly but now, quoting from *Good Health the Natural Way,* Mum insisted this tic could be cured once and for all. To keep the peace I gulped down a morning and evening tonic. Sharon, however, was not interested in the peace. The first time Mum insisted she drink vinegar and honey for her allergies Sharon and I were waiting for a ride to the Odeon Theatre where *National Velvet* was playing.

"I won't," she said. "It's cruelty to children."

"Och, away you go," Mum said. "It'll no kill you."

Sharon said she couldn't drink it even if she wanted to, which she didn't. The smell alone made her want to throw up.

"You'll no be leaving this house until you've taken that drink. Every drop."

As though from a distance I watched Sharon and Mum argue, their hands and mouths moving in an exaggerated manner, their voices coming from a long way off. It was like watching cartoon characters work themselves into a frenzy, the volume turned down. The phone rang in the front hall and Mum left. Sharon jumped up and poured all but a thimbleful of the vinegar and honey down the sink. When Mum came back she looked at Sharon's tumbler and said, "Do you think I came up the Clyde on a bike? Answer me. Do you?"

Sharon squinted defiantly, glasses on the end of her nose.

"I drank mine," I said quietly.

Sharon turned to me and gaped but she lifted the tumbler and took a sip. And then she doubled over and made retching sounds.

Mum said, "You can quit your antics right now."

A car honked in front of the house as Mum yanked Sharon up off the chair and shook her by the shoulders. "You're a bad stick," she said. "A bad, bad stick."

"That's our ride," I said to Mum, but she shook her head. No, Sharon wouldn't be going. I couldn't believe it, nor could I look at Sharon's face. I turned and walked out of the house and slid into the front seat of the car beside my best friend and her mother. For the next two hours I sucked lemon gumdrops in a kind of delirious sweat, watching a girl named Violet win a national horse race, dressed as a boy.

*

BEFORE DAD LEFT, Mum would sing as she washed the dishes. *I belong to Glasgow, dear old Glasgow too-oon.* I'd stand in front of the rack, holding a towel, waiting for the water to drain from the plates.

"Where's Glasgow?" I once asked, and Mum said it was on the River Clyde, the wonderful, wonderful Clyde.

Glasgow was also the home town of the radio talk show host she listened to each afternoon at two o'clock. Jack Webster's voice penetrated every corner of the house. If he agreed with a guest or wanted to sum up a point, he'd say "Pree-cisely," in a loud and exacting way. If he disagreed, he'd say, "Och away you go and dinnee be daft." Just like Mum. The same fierce language.

Before Dad left she cut out a picture of Jack from a magazine and put it inside a little frame above the fridge so she could look at him while he was talking. His face was as gruff as his voice, but Mum liked Jack because, she said, he didn't back down from anyone, no matter how high and mighty they were. He scrapped with union leaders, members of Parliament, even premiers, calling them rogues and scoundrels, the bloody lot of them. At least once during each program he'd quote Robert Burns. *"A Man's a Man for a' that. A Man's a Man for a' that."*

I was at the sink scrubbing beets, hacking off the leaves, when Jack began to interview a woman who'd written a book, *Twenty-Three Years Locked Inside.* Apparently, the woman suffered from a psychological condition that no one, not even psychiatrists, fully understood. She spoke of all the occasions she'd missed because of her condition: picnics and family gatherings, her son's lacrosse games, her neice's wedding.

And the little things she couldn't do: walk to the corner to mail a letter, take a bus into town to buy a new dress. Mum stopped slicing beets into a Mason jar and pulled up a chair. She sat and listened to the woman describe the symptoms she experienced whenever she tried to leave her house — racing heart, panic, sweating, nausea, indescribable dread. My blouse and shorts were sticking to my skin. The air was thick the way it is before thunder.

"People think you're crazy," the woman was saying to Jack. All the lies and secrecy. The shame. Until recently even her husband hadn't known what was wrong with her. "At least prisoners have company," she said.

"Aye," Mum said.

"Aye what?" I said.

"Whisht."

The woman was telling Jack that she'd tried explaining her symptoms to her family doctor but he'd brushed her off and prescribed Valium. "Relax," he'd said. "If you're going to be raped, you might as well lie back and enjoy it."

"Daft bugger," Mum said.

I looked at the beets on the floor. Dirty bouquets wrapped in newspaper. "How many more do I have to wash?" I said.

Mum ignored me and leaned closer to the transistor. The woman was now saying she drank to cope with the anxiety and depression, paying her sons to buy her liquor. She even paid them to not tell their father. Jack, who normally barked questions at his guests, was quiet as the woman related her story of insomnia and dread and wine bottles stashed beneath dirty laundry. Only once did he speak and that was to say, "You're all right, love, I'm listening."

Standing at the kitchen sink, I turned to Mum. Tears were running down her face. When she saw me looking she brought her hand up to her mouth. "I didn't know," she said.

"Know what?"

"I'm no mad."

"Mad?"

"Bammy."

"So."

"There's a name for it. It's got a name." And she pronounced the word the way she might have if she were trying to be funny, imitating a London toff. "Agoraphobia."

A scream ripped the heavy afternoon air and Mum snapped upright. Sharon hopped into the kitchen on one foot, crying, "I stepped in a wasp's nest, I stepped on a zillion wasps." Mum moved across the room, slowly, as though over spongy ground. She opened the fridge and took out an onion.

"There now," she said, "a poultice. To draw out the poison." She and Sharon got down on the floor and she took Sharon's foot in her lap and rubbed the sliced onion on the swollen skin. A local newscaster was now announcing the opening of the Woodward's mall that coming Saturday. Everyone was invited. There'd be balloons, soft drinks, free samples for all. Not only that, The Junk Yard Beats would be playing rock hits from two till four.

"The Junk Yard Beats," Sharon said. "Can we go?"

Mum didn't say yes but for the first time she didn't give an outright no.

*

BEFORE DAD LEFT, I wrote to him constantly.

Dear Dad:

How's construction going?

Sharon and I got scalped at the barber's. Nothing exciting has happened except Mr. Gartrell put the perfect spelling tests (three) on the wall under a sign that says *We Tried Hard.* He put all the other tests under a sign that says *We Will Try Harder.* Ha ha! Mum yelled at Sharon for stealing money from her purse. She bought liquorice gum. It looks like you're chewing black tar. Don't forget to bring me home a present.

Love from your adorable daughter, Gloria.

ps. It starts with H.

Before Dad left he came home with a horse, or, rather, a horse's head on the end of a pole. Now Sharon and I played farmyard in the spare lot beside the house. As the oldest, and the farmer, I gave the orders, but Sharon refused to obey. She wouldn't pick dandelion heads to feed the ducks. The sheep were dying of thirst but she wouldn't fill the metal bucket at the outdoor tap. She'd stamp her feet and wail for her turn to ride Gondola. One morning she kept wailing until Mum stuck her head out a window and shouted, "For the love of god, is there no rest for the wicked?"

"I hate being the wife," Sharon screamed, but Mum had already pulled inside.

"Okay," I said, "but first you have to milk the cows."

And Sharon went berserk, running through the thistles, stomping the fallen plums with the heels of her gumboots.

That night I couldn't sleep. Mosquitoes buzzed around my head, dive bombing my ears and eyes. Earlier, I'd gone into the kitchen to ask Mum to sew my pant leg which had ripped on a nail. I'd gone through the house, calling, and when she didn't answer, Dad and Sharon and I searched all the rooms, checking behind curtains and under beds.

"She's always saying she's going to run away to the Sooke Hills," Dad said, trying to make a joke out of it. Sharon began to cry. "I'm no serious," he said. "You wait and see, we'll find her."

I didn't know where the Sooke Hills were though I did know that members of a religious cult had recently gone there to wait for the end of the world. Mum had read in the newspaper that hundreds of people were camped on the highest hill, believing it would be easier for God to lift them into heaven. I imagined her on a hilltop, surrounded by people in white gowns, a huge hand reaching down from the clouds. Waves of panic passed through me as I rushed frantically around the kitchen, looking inside the fridge and even the bread box. My mouth was dry; my heart was stuck in my throat. I opened the broom closet not expecting to find Mum but there she was huddled in a space with room for only a few mops, a bag of rags and the Hoover. She looked frightened, the way rabbits looked, their nostrils quivering.

"For the love of the wee man," Dad said quietly.

"Away you go," Mum said. "Can you no see I'm trying to get a moment's peace."

Dad closed the door and I tried to imagine other adults sitting on a Hoover in the dark. And then I wondered if I'd just imagined it. Maybe there was no one on the other side of the cupboard door.

Later, Sharon and I stood in front of the little vanity mirror brushing our teeth. Toothpaste foamed over her face and hands, right up to her elbows. Blobs of toothpaste dripped onto the floor.

"Why do you have to make a big production out of everything?" I said.

Sharon spat through a white beard. "It's none of your bloody business."

In bed I kept seeing Mum in the broom closet, Dad's boiler room socks loose around her ankles. The more I thought about it, the farther away the image slid, and still I lay awake. The house creaked as I stole down the stairs and through the kitchen, carrying Gondola. Passing the sunflowers Mum planted every year against the side of the house, I noticed several had been ripped out. The gaps in the dirt looked like spaces in a mouth where teeth had been pulled. The McKeechie boys, I thought. They could never wait.

The sky was deep blue, and everything — the pears hanging from the branches, the tall grass, my own moving legs — seemed shockingly alive, much more alive than in daylight. For a while I cantered around the edge of the lot, whinnying softly, the breeze ruffling my hair. And then the strange light seemed to fill my bones and lift me up. Before Dad left I imagined fantastic things. That Gondola and I would take to the air; we'd fly above the rooftops, girl and horse, and look down on the sleeping city. The few people walking their dogs would look up, amazed, pointing, shaking their heads. Mum, too, would wake and look out her bedroom window — from my perspective, small as a prison cell — and see me soaring above the willow tree, the compost heap, the rabbits who mated day and night, and she'd gasp. "Och aye, there goes Gloria, my own brave lassie."

*

AND THEN DAD LEFT. He left on one of those long golden days at the end of September. He left after making pancakes and crispy bacon, after three cups of cowboy coffee. Living with Mum, he said, was no kind of life. He was sorry for it. He was truly sorry. He'd hoped it would not come to this, but he didn't know which way to turn. At first he'd thought Mum was just high-strung, that she had a bad case of nerves, but it was obviously more than that. And she refused to get help, refused even to go to the doctor despite the fact she knew what ailed her. If it had a name, for Christ's sake, surely it had a cure. Dad said he felt like he was suffocating or losing his mind. Often both. Maybe Mum was better off without him. He said all this while Sharon and I spread plum jam on our pancakes, then cut those pancakes into small pieces and put the pieces into our mouths.

After Dad left, Mum went to her room and closed the blinds. Ear to radio, she might have been someone hunkered down behind the Iron Curtain and Jack Webster might have been the voice of the free world.

On weekends Sharon and I would spend whole days at other people's houses, and beyond, where Blackwood Street tapered off into wild swampy places, we fished with baking sieves, catching things in jars, fluttery things, things that looked back at us with tiny O-shaped mouths and bulging eyes.

After Dad left, the garden turned to weeds and the rabbits ate their young. We learned to negotiate Mum's darkness. And then one day when I was thirteen and Sharon eleven, we came home to find her slicing apples and rolling out pastry, ten aluminum pie plates on the table. With the help of no one, Mum gradually began to ease herself back into some kind of light.

After Dad left she must have cursed her pride and the terrible cage her body had become, but that morning as he stood on the porch, unshaven, hands at his sides, waiting for something — a sign that Mum needed him to stay? — she just slid her fist inside one of Sharon's shoes and began to paint the scuffed toe with whitener.

"No one's holding you," Mum said. "You'd better be off if you're going."

And then she brought the shoe to her lips and blew. For a moment she might have been someone whose world extended beyond the gouged table and scrape of a clothes line. She might have been someone with somewhere to go, a woman who, having just applied nail polish, was blowing it dry.

GARDEN APARTMENT

On the morning of Frank and Nora's departure, Bub wakes with a fever but nothing hurts. Roxy peers into his ears and down his throat. He's a limp doll she prods and rolls this way and that. It's a mystery. He's just hot.

"Maybe it's a blessing," Sam says. "At least no teary goodbyes."

But goodbye all the same. Goodbye Nora. Goodbye Frank.

Sam waits in the car, engine running, while Roxy struggles to balance Bub on one hip and the baby on the other. Frank's knapsack, stuffed with little packets of nuts and raisins, colouring books and felt pens, thumps against his back as he skips across the driveway. "Snorkelling," he hollers, "boogie boarding!" Nora turns on the bottom step and blows a kiss. Pow. A big one for Roxy.

*

WHEN SAM RETURNS from the airport, Roxy's splashing cool water over Bub's back and shoulders. His head lolls, his eyes are glazed. The baby's holding onto the side of the tub, babbling musically. Any minute now, Roxy thinks, the baby's going to launch into full blown speech.

Sam kneels. "Hey," he whispers, "how's it going with you, Bub?"

He wraps Bub in a towel and carries him to the couch where he lies all afternoon, drifting in and out of consciousness. Bub mumbles deliriously, something about ham and honey, an upside down chair. "Ach, ach," he says. "Dirt in my mouth." Every few hours his fever spikes and Roxy sponges him down, feeds him Tylenol and sips of water.

The next morning he comes into the kitchen, wan and subdued, but otherwise fine, asking for his regular breakfast, a soft-boiled egg and Shreddies without milk. Sam and Roxy look at each other as though to say, Crisis Averted.

And then Bub starts toward the basement door.

"Frank's gone," Roxy says. "He left yesterday. Remember, they went to live in Hawaii."

Bub rolls his eyes as though Roxy's the four-year-old. "I know that," he says. "I just want to see if he forgot any toys."

*

ROXY'S ON THE PHONE when she feels her bones hollow out; cold sand rushes through them. It's a chilling sensation: her body knows something she doesn't. She hears her voice say, "I have to go." She watches the phone slip from her hand. On the back deck she leans over the railing and words leave her mouth. "Bub. Gone." Words that sound like someone gasping for breath. Standing in the vegetable garden, Sam squints up at her, chewing on a piece of grass. "Damn deer ate the spinach."

Roxy says it again. "Bub's gone."

"I just saw him," Sam says. "He's around here somewhere."

"Weren't you watching him?"

"I thought you were."

A high-pitched whine fills Roxy's head and she wonders how she has arrived at this place, at this time, arguing with a man she suddenly despises about a missing child. From his face, she can see he's wondering the same thing.

*

LAST FALL SAM was working construction and Roxy was part-time at the florists, but it was never enough. They were living on Visa, their line of credit. Every few months they'd talk half-heartedly about fixing up the basement, renting to a couple of students. All their neighbours were doing the same thing; the suburb was a hotbed of illegal suites. And then the transmission blew on the car, the roof started to leak.

Roxy, in her seventh month, said, "Let's do it, Sam. We can do it on the cheap."

They drove out to *The House Wreckers*, a demo place on the highway, and bought a pink toilet, a blue bathtub, an avocado sink. "Mexican decor," Roxy said. "All the crazy colours."

A few weeks later, Sam had cobbled together a rudimentary kitchen and bathroom, framed in a living room and two small bedrooms. While he was at work, Roxy painted the walls and then wrote the ad for the university newspaper — *Garden apartment, five minute walk to campus, utils. inc.*

"Garden apartment?" Sam said. "Isn't that false advertising?"

Roxy pointed to the raspberry current bush in the corner of the yard and reminded him that frilly flowers would blossom next spring.

"You don't look so good," Sam said. "Maybe you should lie down."

Roxy was retaining water. The doctor'd told her to stay off her feet and sometimes she did. The following afternoon when Sam showed the suite to an array of prospective tenants, she was lying on the bed like a beached whale.

"So what're they like?" she said later.

"Real nice," Sam said. "Frank's Bub's age, and Nora, well, she seems responsible."

"Responsible's good," Roxy said. "Responsible is very good."

"In her fourth year. Anthropology. Says it's the one true discipline."

Roxy rubbed her hands. "Now the money's gonna start rolling in."

Standing in the doorway, smoking his last ever cigarette, Sam didn't look so convinced. "Something about this," he said. "It doesn't feel right."

Roxy was poking around in the fridge. Pregnant with Bub, she'd craved Bernstein's Oil and Vinegar Dressing, sometimes even drinking straight from the bottle. This time she wanted starch — rice pudding and oily pasta, thick slabs of white bread and peanut butter. Forty-five pounds later, she'd puffed out like a puffer fish.

"Frank?" she said. "Who names their kid Frank?"

"Seven hundred bucks," Sam said. "It's a lot of money for a shitty little basement suite."

"Hey," Roxy said. "There's nothing shitty about it."

"We could drop the rent," Sam said. "She *is* a single mum."

Roxy could feel Sam watching as she snapped the lid off a plastic container. She scooped cold lumpy potatoes into her mouth and swallowed quickly. "A bud for Bub," she said, and then for no reason, she said it again.

*

ROXY WATCHED NORA carry a box of books into the basement, then return to stand in the driveway, hands on her hips, assessing all her worldly possessions. She was young, not more than twenty-five, and wearing a white peasant blouse and faded jeans. Her long black hair coiled down her back like a strip of shiny liquorice. Silver bracelets rattled half way up one arm.

"Cramp," Roxy said, reaching for the back of a love seat.

"I envy you!" Nora said enthusiastically. "Giving birth is such a high!"

Sam bounding down the steps with Roxy's overnight bag. "Let's get this show on the road," he said, and it flashed through her mind that she'd been tricked, that good, kind Sam had tricked her; he might have said *something* about Nora's exotic willowy beauty. Roxy waited for the pain to pass, then started toward the car, feeling bigger and more hideous than she'd felt during her entire pregnancy. It was late November, frost on the grass, her ankles and feet so swollen she was wearing Sam's plastic beach thongs.

Nora called after her: "Wish I could do it for you! I mean that! I just loved having Frank!"

Roxy half turned to say, I'm so glad for you, but Nora was heading back into the basement, a cedar basket balanced on her head.

*

STUCK IN THE birth canal, the baby was born with a cone-shaped head and a bad case of jaundice. Right away Roxy and Sam started calling her China Bean. One nurse said, "Yellow skin's common in newborns. Think California tan." Another said, "If the bilirubin goes much higher she'll need a blood transfusion." Sam stood beside Roxy's bed, breathing heavily through his nose, a sign he was troubled and thinking. Across the street the Catholic girl's school, recently boarded up, looked like the set of a gothic movie.

"I've called a few sitters for Bub," he said. "And I can ask Nora to help out."

What could Roxy say? Really, what *could* she say? She wasn't the type to dislike someone just because they possessed a heart-shaped face and birdlike bones. For the next six days she did crossword puzzles and read Robert Ludlum novels. In the nursery she watched her masked baby sleep beneath the billy lights, legs pulled up like a large toad. Roxy took sitz baths and wandered the halls. Each time she passed a laundry cart and smelled the fresh linen she was overcome with inexplicable longings. In the maternity lounge, flipping through an old *Reader's Digest,* she read an article about a mother of five who yearned to pursue a spiritual path. When the woman complained to the Dalai Lama about all the cooking and cleaning and laundry, he said, "Your children are your path. Relate to them as though each one is a Buddha."

And then Sam phoned to say Nora's sink was clogged, he wouldn't be able to make it up for visiting hours. In fact, he was shoving the sewer snake into the drain as he spoke.

"Here," he said to Roxy, "talk to Bub."

"Hey, Bub," she said, "I'm coming home tomorrow with your baby sister."

But Bub wasn't interested. All he could talk about was Frank and Nora. She'd promised to take him to Open House at the University Daycare. "They've got jungle gym," Bub said, breathlessly. "And popcorn."

*

DEER MOVED LIKE four-legged apparitions through the misty field, lifting their hooves daintily, as though to avoid touching the wet grass. The sun rose, fierce and red, as Roxy drifted off in the rocker, China Bean asleep at her breast. She woke to Bub pressed against the window, watching Nora and Frank walk hand and hand along the footpath, their bright yellow slickers retreating into the trees bordering the university ring road. They disappeared and Bub let out a sad little cry. All morning he whined and sulked and refused to entertain himself. When Roxy sat to nurse the baby again, he lay at her feet, thumping his head on the floor. Her milk wouldn't let down and China Bean kept shrieking and arching her back.

"Stop that," Roxy said to Bub. "If you don't stop that right now, so help me I will." Bub raised his head and looked at her curiously. That afternoon she was back at the window, still in her nightgown, watching a group of Biology students tramp across the field towards Rickets Bog to join the bird-watchers with their binoculars and notebooks. And then Frank and Nora emerged from the trees, swinging their arms. It looked like they were singing. How dare they, Roxy thought, her throat tasting of bile. The phone rang beneath her, three, four, five times, and then Frank, like a bird rustled up from the forest floor, burst into the kitchen, calling for Bub.

*

NORA ASKED ROXY to babysit. She'd been invited to a gathering of students interested in studying abroad. "Abroad!" she said. "Just a small gathering!" Everything she said seemed to be punctuated with an exclamation point and yet, Roxy thought, there was a strange disconnect about Nora. Her voice went up while her expression remained neutral. The following week Nora asked Roxy to babysit again and soon it became habit. Frank would sleep in Bub's bed and the next morning Sam would make waffles and take the boys to the pool. Sometime in the afternoon Nora would phone, groggy and hungover.

"Send Frank down whenever you like!"

At Christmas break, Nora and Frank flew to Dawson City and Bub moped at the top of the stairs like an abandoned dog. Sam would offer to play soccer in the backyard or street hockey in the carport, but Bub would just shake his head. Two weeks later, on a drizzly morning, Roxy was reading to Bub on the couch, the same stupifyingly dull book over and over — *Big Joe's Trailer Truck* — afraid of what she might do if Bub again insisted she stop at the double-page spread at the end so he could name, with painstaking deliberateness, every part of Joe's rig, and then she heard a car. Thank god. Nora and Frank were getting out of a cab in front of the house. With his coifed hair and navy Burberry, Frank looked like a miniature playboy.

"My savior!" Roxy said, and jumped up to open the door.

Nora flipped through her mail and chatted about her mother, half Dene, Roxy learned, while Frank and Bub circled each other shyly. Bub was so excited he started stuttering the way he'd stuttered when he'd first learned to talk. China Bean was lying on a blanket on the floor, a helium balloon tied to her ankle. With every kick, the disembodied clown face jerked and wobbled above her. Nora'd had her hair cut and looked terrific and Roxy told her so. Sam said it was a shame.

"Shame," Roxy snapped. "Why shame?"

"It was nice hair," he said. "That's all."

*

SAM WAS ALWAYS making improvements at Nora's request. He put up a pot rack in her kitchen, a vanity mirror in her bathroom. One night after dinner he went down to work on a clothes closet and Roxy flung a Cheerio box across the living room. Tiny Os scattered. She imagined Sam in Nora's bedroom, pencil between his teeth, Nora passing him the tape measure, a level.

The night before Sam's hand had moved up the inside of Roxy's thigh and she'd gritted her teeth and imagined diving into ice cold water. She loved Sam but she felt used up. Mauled. "No hands," she'd wanted to scream, "no more hands."

Roxy and Sam hadn't made love since the baby's birth, a problem, she knew, but a problem she couldn't seem to get around. Sex had become strange to her. Bodies had become strange. Sam's. Her own. She'd stand naked in front of the mirror, horrified and incredulous. She'd always been a big woman but big in the best sense, big as in strong, with long shapely legs and clearly defined muscles. How to recognize herself inside this body, these milk-engorged breasts, this doughy stomach?

She walked back and forth, grinding cereal beneath her heels, thinking: asexual, non-sexual, sexless, unsexed, de-sexed. What was she? What had she become? Through the air vents, she could hear Nora and Sam laughing. His electric drill bit into wood and the word riven came to mind. We are riven, Roxy thought. Riven.

*

THE GARDEN APARTMENT smelled sour and cloying; it smelled of sex. Roxy crept past Nora's closed bedroom door and stepped through the glass beads hanging in the kitchen doorway, surprised to see Nora curled up in her nook, legs tucked inside a bulky red sweater. She looked puffy-eyed but also adorable in a tousled sort of way. Across from her sat a rumpled man with deep grey eyes and a mass of grey curls. Roxy stammered something about eggs, Bub and Frank wanting pancakes, and Nora leapt up and squeezed past her, pulling a carton out of the fridge.

"Here, take these!"

Roxy could smell the man on Nora, the fried food and cigarette smoke, the years of bad living absorbed into the sweater's wool. All day Roxy wondered who he was. One of Nora's profs? Did she go for old guys? Once, Roxy had asked about Frank's father and Nora'd looked at her as though she'd said something tactless. As though she'd crossed a line. Roxy and Nora didn't talk about the things women talked about — love and men and sex — which was odd, Roxy thought, because she was sure Nora talked to Sam about such things. And why not? Sam was a good listener; he somehow opened himself up to people without saying a word. And he exuded a delicious kind of energy. Just being around him made you feel as though something a little bit exciting was about to happen.

Roxy would hear Sam and Nora talking in the laundry room or out by the garbage cans — Nora's animated voice, Sam's deep murmurings — and wonder what they were saying. But she never asked. She didn't like to imply anything improper. She didn't like to insinuate. The sound of jealousy could turn anyone, even someone as big as Roxy, into something very small.

*

ON THE BEACH, kids were throwing bread crusts into the air. Gulls swooped, breasts lit with gold. China Bean was in the carrier on Roxy's back and Bub was on a swing. Beside her, Nora pushed Frank.

"Harder," the boys shouted, both of them pumping and screaming each time their chains buckled. The air smelled of kelp and wild roses and for the first time in a long time Roxy felt hopeful and rooted to the ground.

For three weeks she'd been living on water and brown rice and grapefruit and that morning for the first time she'd managed to get into her old Levis. She couldn't fully exhale, but the jeans seemed an amazing accomplishment, the first step to some kind of future. Nora was saying that Frank had accused her of flushing Bo Diddly, his favourite puppet, down the toilet because he dreams things, she said, then thinks they really happened!

Roxy laughed. "Me too. Me too." She felt so relaxed she confessed to Nora that she fantasized about belonging to a professional association some day. It didn't matter which one. She fantasized about having colleagues and deadlines and coffee dates and pay stubs and phone messages with Urgent! scrawled across them.

"That's so weird," Nora said. "I don't know anyone who wants those things! Honestly, I don't!"

A small olive-skinned boy ran toward the swings and stopped at the edge of the asphalt. "My brother says to tell you he thinks you're foxy ladies."

Nora laughed. "Tell your brother in his dreams!"

Roxy turned to the tennis courts where a couple of boys raised their rackets in gentlemanly salutes. High school, college? The small boy stood for a moment, repeating Nora's words to himself, then turned and ran.

Roxy said, "He was just giving you a compliment."

"Don't be coy," Nora said, "he was giving you one too!"

*

"How's it going with you, Roxy-Girl?" Sam said, nuzzling her neck.

"It's going good," she said. "It's going just fine." And right then it was. Right then, Roxy was feeling terrific. It was Friday and all the doors and windows were open. The fruit trees, full of chirping birds, were waving their new leaves, and downstairs Nora was making margaritas in her blender. Since coming home Sam had kissed Roxy three times, long deep kisses, and now he was chopping onions and oinking and quacking along with China Bean. And then Nora was standing between Sam and Roxy, holding out salt-rimmed glasses and saying tuition to law school in Hawaii was going to cost an arm and a leg, but, hey, who needed two arms and two legs. Sam's knife slipped, China Bean shrieked ba-aa-aa, and blood was everywhere. Nora grabbed a dish towel and Roxy ran to look for gauze and bandages in the medicine cabinet. When she returned, Sam's index finger was bound in the cotton scarf which only moments before had been knotted around Nora's neck.

Finally they all sat.

Sam wasn't hungry, he said, but would Nora mind making him another margarita with an extra shot of tequila? She slumped forward, elbows on the table, and pouted.

"Poor didums!" she said. "Did woo hurt wore widdel finger?"

Baby talk? Nora? Roxy was stunned. Nora didn't talk silly even to Frank. Nora left and Roxy daubed refried beans onto the boys' tortillas, then watched Frank spread his beans thinly and precisely to the edge of the circle. He rolled his tortilla into a neat little log, took a small bite and wiped his lips with his napkin. Bub was stuffing food into his mouth, beans and cheese and tomatoes spilling down the front of his shirt. When Nora returned with Sam's margarita, she said she didn't have much of an appetite either. She guessed all the blood! She sat beside him and picked a clove of garlic from the bowl in the centre of the table and began to talk about an installation artist she knew who ate a head of raw garlic every day. Roxy tried to concentrate while watching Nora peel the papery skin, but she couldn't, nothing made sense. Why had Sam's knife slipped right at that moment? Why were Frank and Bub and China Bean, all three of them, silent for the first time ever? Why was Nora talking about an installation artist who ate garlic cloves like candy? And then Sam said, "How can you go from Anthropology to Law?"

"People do!" Nora said. "They do it all the time!"

Bub and Frank slurped the last of their chocolate milk, then got up and bumped into each other, eyes closed, pretending to be blind mice.

China Bean started to squawk in her seat so Roxy picked her up and walked around the table.

"Installation artists are all about the ephemeral nature of beauty!" Nora said as the baby spat up and Roxy reached for a napkin, wiping the milk from her shoulder. She looked at the strip of flycatcher dangling from the ceiling, a few legs and wings still moving.

"They want us to *drink in* the moment!" Nora said, and closed her eyes as though she were doing just that.

*

AN HOUR LATER Roxy walked past the window, China Bean on her hip, and saw Nora and the rumpled-looking man standing face to face in the driveway. Nora's arms were crossed defiantly across her chest. The man, towering over her, was gesturing wildly. A lovers' spat? Was he also upset she was leaving? He turned abruptly and started toward the silver Audi parked on the street, his long raincoat flapping against his legs, and then he swung round and came back and grasped Nora's head in his hands. He stared at her for a long moment, then pulled her to him, swallowing her up in his huge body.

Roxy stepped away from the window, confused and embarrassed. She couldn't remember. Had Sam ever wanted her that much? Had she ever wanted him? She sat in the rocker and blew lightly on China Bean's face. The baby laughed, eyelashes aflutter, and Roxy blew again. It was a game they played before each feeding now. When finally China Bean latched on, a huge and formless longing welled up in Roxy, and she had the sensation of coming violently apart. China Bean stopped to look around, hyper-alert, and Roxy guided her back, but the baby stopped again. After a few more tries Roxy gave up.

On the way down the hall she glanced into the den, dark except for the flashing TV screen, and saw Sam's hand with the bandaged finger resting on Nora's thigh. But when Roxy looked again Nora wasn't there and Bub was curled up on Sam's lap. "What's going on?" Roxy said to China Bean. "This is my life and I don't know what's going on."

*

IN A BURST OF MOTION Sam runs across the back yard and up the steps, grabbing his keys off the hook by the door. His face is ghoulish white. "You walk," he says to Roxy, "I'll drive." The car's wheels spit gravel in the driveway as she buckles the baby into the stroller and carries it down the steps and starts calling to anyone she sees — the teenagers hanging off the side of a porch, the old woman watching a naked child run through a sprinkler, the man into whose backyard she barges because she doesn't know what else to do. He's been dozing in a lounge chair, but now sits up, blinking. "Bub? No Bub here."

Has anyone seen a little boy — this big, chunky body, sandy hair, blue T-shirt, running shoes, gap between his front teeth? Roxy doesn't wait for answers because she knows none of these people have seen Bub, though it would have taken only a kind word and the shake of a Smarties box to lure him into any one of these oil-stained garages.

Up one street and down another. A dead end. A cul de sac. Which way? The suburb is a maze. Every house and car and tree's identical, washed out, soulless. And then it hits her. Frank! Bub's gone to look for Frank. Right now he's trekking through the fields toward the university, the way he saw Frank and Nora go each morning of the university term. Roxy's heart stops beating. She can't breathe. So, this is how it will be for the rest of her life, this is what it is to exist without a heartbeat or breath, thank god, without a heartbeat or breath she will die soon.

She swings the stroller back toward the house, cursing Frank the whole way. How sinister he seems now, his exquisite table manners and designer clothes, a lisping devil's boy, barely human. She curses Nora. Everything she knows about her and everything she doesn't. She curses Sam for renting to Nora. How blind could he be? Any fool could see Nora would bring nothing but grief. Roxy curses herself for wanting the money. Her greed has brought this nightmare upon them. Fuck the overdraft. Fuck the mortgage. A trapdoor opens and she's falling through a stagnant world of black orchids and carnivorous tentacles.

Rickets Bog!

Back home she dials 9-1-1 and within minutes a young police officer is sitting in the kitchen, writing on a pad: Bub's clothing, his physical characteristics. Roxy itemizes everything she can think of, including his protruding belly button.

"Any idea why Jeremy might have wandered off?" the officer asks.

"Bub,"Roxy says. "Actually, we call him Bub. He's gone to look for Frank."

"And where can we find this Frank?"

"Manoa."

"Manoa?"

"In Hawaii."

He looks down at his notepad, then back at Roxy: "Okay, let's start again."

By the time Sam returns, a search party's been mobilized across the street, preparing to scour the fields and woods around the university. He leaves to join it and Roxy sits on the kitchen floor and rolls a tennis ball to China Bean who tries to roll it back. Rickets Bog, Roxy thinks, then looks up at the clock. Bog. Ball. She checks her watch. Rolls the ball. What exactly *is* a bog? The ball. Her watch. Can you get bogged down in a bog? Clock. Ball. Watch. Is it like quicksand? Can you get sucked in?

The phone rings but Roxy can't lift her hand; it's a dead weight. And then she realizes China Bean's screaming so she picks up the phone and it's the officer, the same one, saying, "Good news, real good news. Your boy's fine. He's just fine. Call just came in. He's at the *Kentucky Fried Chicken* at Shelborne and Cedar Hill."

Roxy can't speak.

"Seems he went in to order himself a chicken dinner."

She imagines speeding trucks, semis, four lane traffic, intersections. And Bud hates walking. He *hates* it.

"But how?" she says. "Why?"

"Hungry!" The officer sounds as giddy as Roxy feels. "Guess the little guy got the hungries."

*

A MUSCLE CAR screeches to a stop at the corner, revs up, then tears off again. Roxy and Sam drag a couple of kitchen chairs out to the deck along with their beers. It's after eleven and starting to rain. Through the metal railings she can see chalk butterflies on the pavement, enormous mauve and yellow wings. By morning they'll be washed away. Beauty. Its ephemeral nature.

"Every time I think," Sam says.

"Don't," Roxy says. "Don't even go there."

The music student in the neighbour's basement is tuning his violin. A searchlight sweeps the summer sky. Everything changed, Roxy thinks, then changed again. Bub disappeared into a black hole but now he's sleeping in his bed. She and Sam looked at each other, pure loathing in their eyes, but now they look at each other and smile and smile.

"I'm going to miss Frank," she says.

"He was a neat kid," Sam says.

"What about Nora? Think you'll miss her?"

Sam shrugs.

"What was the deal with her anyhow?" Roxy says.

"Nora?"

"Yeah. Nora."

"What deal?"

"You were always talking. She never talked to me like that."

"Like what?"

"Like, I don't know. *Talking*."

"There was no deal."

"No?"

"No."

With his index finger Sam draws an X on his chest. And that's enough for Roxy. At least right now it's enough, it's more than enough because she and Sam have walked through fire together and arrived at this place, purged and cleansed, their heads tipped back, rain on their faces, beer in their mouths. She can smell the tang of wet pavement.

"Three kilometres," he says.

"Over three," she says.

"Who'd believe it?"

"No one."

"Hey, we're whispering."

"We *are* whispering," Roxy says. She has no idea why.

80

AIRSTREAM

Dill pedals slowly down the middle of the street and Trudy jogs alongside. She hates going to the Bank Street house, the filthy toilets and rotting garbage, the police always kicking in doors, but Dill promises they won't stay. He just wants his money. He lifts his bike up the steps and onto the wrap-around porch, kneels to fiddle with the lock.

Trudy rocks on her heels. "This place is so nasty," she says.

"Three hundred bucks," Dill says. "Kent owes me. If I don't get it now."

The front door's boarded up so she starts toward the side entrance, but Dill steps in front of her, his face suddenly serious. "Just so you know," he says, "I'm going to watch."

"Watch?"

"Yeah. Watch."

"Watch what?"

"Watch Kent."

"Watch Kent what?"

"Jeeze, Trude, sometimes you can be so dense."

"Watch Kent shoot up?"

"It's not like I want to or anything." Dill says this with quick shakes of his head. "They say it helps your resolve. It affirms your conviction."

"What does that even mean?"

"It's good for me, Trude. It means this is good."

He lays his hands on her shoulders and her body goes loose. Their foreheads touch and she's raw with it, skinless, turned inside out, despite his addiction, because of it, she doesn't know, doesn't know anything anymore, just that she'll do whatever it takes because he's Dill and she's Trudy, they're Trudy and Dill, two halves of a whole, and he understands her better than anyone and that's all that matters.

81

"But you said for sure this time," she says.

"Listen to what I'm telling you! It's going to make me strong."

"Bullshit."

"It's no big deal, Trude. I'm just going to go in, get my money, watch Kent do his thing, and then come right back out and we'll do whatever you want." He flicks his fingers. Fffft. fffft. In. Out. The door opens and Kent's standing in the hall, jeans but no shirt. He's pale and glassy-eyed.

"You said wait so I did," he says.

"Five minutes," Trudy says to Dill. "I mean it." She holds up a hand. "Five."

*

LAST SEPTEMBER Dill sat on the edge of his bed, holding his head in his hands while Trudy tapped on the window to get the cat's attention.

"Stop," he groaned. "Christ."

She tapped again. She tapped louder. Dill looked flushed, miserable. The cat licked a paw then drew the paw across its face. Above, in the kitchen, the Hungarian cook turned on faucets and closed cupboard doors.

"What's wrong with you?" Trudy said. "You've been acting weird all day."

"Sit." He patted the space beside him on the bed, but she stayed where she was. And then he said it. He just said it like he was saying he needed a new toothbrush or his shoelace had broken. He said, "I'm a junkie, Trude."

The cat meowed. The cook sang.

"Junkie?" They stared at each other. "So you like to get high. Who doesn't?"

He shook his head. "It's more than that. I'm really fucked up."

She made a face and sort of lunged at him playfully. "You're saying you'll go berserko if you don't get it?"

"Don't do that." There were tears in his eyes.

"Hey. You're serious."

Above them, the cook clickety-clacked back and forth across the hardwood floors in high heel sandals, the cat yowled beneath the window, and Trudy flashed back to all the times Dill had disappeared from parties, then turned up hours later with some feeble excuse. The mysterious cars that appeared out of nowhere. The times, returning to school after lunch, when he'd make a quick detour around back to meet Kent in the smoking pit. She kneeled in front of him.

"I quit," he said. "I'm just telling you so you know."

It was 1972, a slate grey sky. Face down on a bedside table: a Math 11 textbook, a copy of *The Turn of the Screw*. Sweet and sour spareribs bubbling in the oven. Next year Dill would be dead but that afternoon Trudy could hear the rush of his heart and the cook's voice as it wound down to a wordless humming. And then the cat hurled itself against the glass.

*

FOR THE NEXT few months Trudy couldn't keep track. Was Dill using, wasn't he, was he, wasn't he? "What's with all the secrecy?" she said. "I thought it was you and me. I thought we were in this together."

"I've told you everything. There's nothing else."

"That creepy drug house. It's so fucking creepy."

He and Kent did things without her. Concerts in Vancouver. In the middle of the week they'd skip school and drive up to Nanaimo in Kent's mum's Jag. Trudy and Dill fought, fists and everything — once she drew blood. At the beginning of Christmas break, he flew to Banff to be with his sisters and mother but instead of skiing he spent two weeks in bed. Flu, he said, and his mother believed him. When Trudy picked him up at the airport the first thing he said was, "I did it, Trude, I'm clean."

For the first weeks of January they tried to act the way they imagined normal teenagers would act. Trudy made muffins and tea and they did their homework at her kitchen table. But she could feel it; Dill was somewhere else, plotting, making plans. He smoked and stared out the window, ignoring the books open around him.

"Algebra used to be so easy," he said. "Didn't I used to ace this algebra shit?"

*

THEY ARGUED all the time. Trudy hated what they'd become. After big fights they'd make up in the Airstream on Dill's father's property, beneath layers of quilts, the wind blasting the trailer as though it were a flimsy tin can. One night in March, Kent knocked on the door and they scrambled into clothes. An hour later, sitting around the little mahogany table, drinking beer and talking, Kent and Dill were best buddies again, but Trudy was suffocating. The air inside the trailer was packed with poisonous bubbles, which she imagined stabbing with the letter opener in the mug behind Dill's head. The trailer was full of souvenirs from New Mexico — stone pestle, bird's nest, walking stick. Stuff Dill's parents had collected when they were still together.

He slid off the bench and opened the little fridge.

"Bad news, my friends, no more brewskies."

"Your dad's stocked," Kent said. Beneath the table, his knee vibrated.

Through the open door Trudy watched Dill run across the lawn in socks, wishing she were anywhere but where she was, even at home, reading with her elderly parents in their gloomy living room. She took the ostrich egg down from a shelf and spread her hands around the thick ivory shell. Kent flicked his lighter on and off.

"Let's see if you like fire as much as eggs."

He reached across the table and held the flame under her chin. Her hand flew up and knocked the lighter across the trailer. The egg hit the floor.

"Oops," Kent said.

"Way to be a jerk. Dill loved that egg."

Dill came back with a half empty whiskey bottle and Kent said, "We had a little accident." He leaned over and picked up a few pieces of broken eggshell. No one spoke and then finally Dill said, "What's the deal? No one died here. It was just a fucking egg."

When the whiskey was gone, Kent said he was going to Bank Street. Was anyone else coming?

"No," Trudy said.

"Sure?" Kent said.

"Very," Trudy said.

"Going going gone."

After Kent left, she said, "He tried to burn me."

Dill shrugged.

"I *said* he tried to burn me. See." She tipped back her head.

"Come on, Trude."

"You weren't here. You didn't see."

"He's a goof," Dill said. "He just likes to goof around."

"I know goofing around."

"What do you want me to say? He tried to set you on fire? Are you happy now, Joan of Arc?"

"Why do you always stick up for him?"

"You liked him before."

"That was before. Things were different before." She stood to put on her jean jacket. As she reached behind her head to yank out her hair, Dill said, "You going too?"

"Don't sound so disappointed."

"Christ, Trude."

"Now you can go out and score."

"What do you know about being strung out? You think you know everything, but what do you know?"

*

DILL IN SUNGLASSES, riding a yellow bike. Trudy in running shoes, jogging alongside. They travelled all over the city like that, down side streets at two in the morning, through parking lots at dawn. Inseparable. Always in motion. The gardens lushly alive, the trees on the boulevards weighed down with sweetly pungent blossoms the colour of boysenberry ice-cream.

Once, after rain, Dill's front wheel skidded on the oily pavement and he fell off. Trudy reached out to help but he said no. Cutting through the golf course, she tried to kiss him but he shrank back. She stuffed a handful of grass down the front of his shirt and he pushed her away.

"Fuck off."

"Fuck off yourself."

She stomped ahead, ankle-length cape flapping against her legs.

"Not one true friend," he shouted after her. "Not one true friend in the whole damn world."

*

TRUDY PICKS synthetic burrs off the couch, and then flicks the little fuzz balls into the air. If she did this solidly for an hour, attacking one cushion only, there'd still be more. A mindless pastime, though she is grateful for it.

The light on the porch is a dappled underwater green. Beyond the massive chestnut tree in front of the house, the sun inches across the sky. Fist-sized warts cover the trunk. A boy with long greasy hair is telling her that all the trees on Bank Street are rotten at the core and will have to come down soon. He tells her the ugly couch she's sitting on once belonged to Bob Denver of Gilligan's Island, which, Trudy thinks, would be impressive if it were true. When the boy goes inside the screen door slams and a girl's voice cries, "Gimme a hug."

Trudy looks at her watch. Twenty minutes and still no sign of Dill. She realizes she doesn't know how long it takes to shoot up. What does it involve? Dill's never offered any information and she's never found a way to ask. His drug life and her. He keeps them separate.

A girl is moving past the fence slats in sandals and a short flouncy skirt. "Greetings earthling," she says. On the top step she stands for a moment: big-boned, blonde ringlets, a high forehead. Kind of beautiful in a German fairy tale way. "This porch is so cool," she says. "Like we should be drinking mint juleps or something." She pauses. "What is a mint julep?"

"Bourbon," Trudy says. Dill's father made mint juleps the summer before, then drank so many he started going on about what a great guy Mussolini was, getting Italy back to work.

"Mint too, I guess," the girl says in a husky voice. Her eyebrows arch knowingly as she looks at the house, and then wags a finger as though she's already scolding some boy fixing in a dirty room.

*

"CLOSE YOUR EYES," Dill says, "be still."

Half-light and birdsong, the sluice of waves. The window of Trudy's bedroom is open. Lying on her back, she's so still she can hear a popping sound, like the sound of broom pods at the end of August, a sound that might be coming from inside her head. She hears her mother in the next yard, explaining to the neighbour that it's not his day to water his lawn.

"Wednesdays and Sundays," she's saying. "Twice a week."

"Imagine we slept together all night," Dill says. "That it's morning. Imagine we're just waking up."

Trudy opens her eyes. "Yeah. Morning. It could be."

For a while they lie in the dusky attic room beneath the sloping roof, pretending they're older, that this is their bed, in their apartment, in some other city. It's an exciting idea. Trudy turns and lays a hand on Dill's cheek, surprised as always by the stubbly feeling, the whiskers so invisible his face appears smooth as a girl's.

"When do you think we'll do it?" she says.

They've talked about birth control before — should she go on the pill, will he use a condom, and what about foam, does it really work? For months she's insisted she's not ready and he's agreed — "What's the rush anyhow?" — but the fact is, she is ready, she's never been more ready for anything in her life. Dill yanks up her shirt and plants a wet kiss on her stomach. She moans and pulls him on top, wanting the weight of him, wanting him closer, deeper, whatever that means. He pins her arms on either side of her head, his knee easing hers apart.

"Admit it," he says, "you're helpless."

"I am. I'm helpless." It feels like her whole body is smiling.

Her mother's voice, impatient and closer, is no longer in the neighbour's yard. "There's a water shortage, for godsake. It's not a free-for-all, you know."

"Not here," Trudy says. "Not now."

*

87

IN THE MARBLE foyer of Dill's house, she steps around five prone bodies. "Vogue Posse," a voice says from above. Girls are half-sitting, half-lying on the stairs leading up to the main living area. Trudy bends over a body and pokes a shoulder to see if it's alive. "Horse tranquilizer," the voice says, "the whole posse took it."

On the back deck, Trudy finds Dill. His eyes are bright and unfocused. "You don't need to follow me around," he says, "because I'm good, we're good. Just relax. It's a party. Hey, it *is* a party. I'll get you a beer." He leaves and Trudy watches a girl in the driveway jerking spasmodically beneath the basketball hoop. Trudy doesn't recognize the dancer, doesn't recognize anyone. These are mostly Kent's private school friends. When Dill doesn't come back, she goes inside and wanders around, sticking her head into rooms, trying not to look for him, but looking anyway. Such a big empty house, seven bedrooms, five bathrooms, a tennis court, a saltwater pool. Dill told her he chose to stay with his dad because he thought they'd start doing stuff together, normal dad and son stuff — camping, watching sports on TV, playing golf. He was twelve. He loved the idea of having his dad to himself.

In the billiard room Dill and Kent are chalking their cues, racking balls. Kent looks great, like he's just stepped out of a commercial for breath mints. Two months ago his parents kidnapped him and when he came back he was different. He was clean.

"Hey, Trude," Kent says, but Dill ignores her; he won't meet her eye. He sinks an impossible corner ball then throws his cue on the table.

"You two play," he says. "I need some air."

*

ONE BEER, TWO, THREE. Trudy downs them fast. From the top of the stairs she watches the Posse return clumsily to life. A girl with a baby face and pillow-soft breasts raises her head and says something about the mariachi, that it will never be the same. She puts on her glasses and gets up and lurches out the door and down the sloping front lawn, arms and legs going in opposite directions. Beneath an oak tree, she collapses and lies on her back, a broken toy.

The living room's packed with people talking and dancing. A glass wall faces the sea. A tiled fireplace takes up another. There's no furniture in the room except for the baby grand, which looks like it's made of white chocolate. Dill's plunking away with one hand, a version of "Satisfaction," the ash on his cigarette growing longer and longer. He grinds the cigarette into the keys, and then bangs down a fist and the room falls silent. He swings around, head panning the room.

"So, what's it like being the beautiful people?"

A few laughs. A few groans. Someone says, "Fuck you, Dill."

"You," he says. "And you. And you. All the beautiful people." He looks at Trudy. "All the beautiful people and their beautiful fucking lives." Then Kent's beside her, saying he's making a run to the jar store, does she want to come? She looks at Dill. Then Kent. Dill. Yes, she does.

*

IN THE LIQUOR STORE parking lot they find a boot who, for a couple of bucks, buys them five cases of *Lucky*. With his teeth, Kent opens two bottles for the road. He takes the long way back to the party, following the coast, windows open, and for a moment everything seems easy, no second guessing, no surprise twists.

"I'm going to get so wasted I won't remember any of this tomorrow," Trudy shouts above the wind and music blasting from the speakers. Kent laughs and she laughs too because it's summer and she's here, in this city, in this life, cruising past the marina, its forest of masts, and not at Dill's, watching him hate her, and then Kent's turning the corner, putting the car into neutral, turning off the ignition. They coast down the street until the Jag runs out of momentum and stops, and it's funny just sitting there, staring at Dill's house and beyond, the Juan de Fuca Strait, the Cascade Mountains, but she's not going to speak because that's what Kent wants, and then he reaches over and delicately pulls a long hair from her sweater.

"Another beer?" He turns to blow the hair out the window.

They sit in the middle of the road, drinking and talking about people at the party, avoiding the subject of Dill, what he said in the billiard room, his bizarre rant at the piano, and then Trudy can't stand it, she needs to defend him, even to Kent.

"He went to the drug clinic," she says. "Plus, he's going to see a counsellor once a week."

"Yeah," Kent says, "that's cool."

"It is," she says.

"Relax. I'm agreeing with you."

And then Kent tells her about the nightmare he had before going into rehab. "I'm running in a field alongside a cruise ship, and everyone's on it, my mum and dad and brothers and sister, even my grandparents, and they're all waving at me. If I run fast enough, I'll be able to catch up, but then the ground goes soft and mud's oozing through my toes. I'm up to my knees in it, I'm sinking fast, and then I just give up. And it hits me, they're both the same thing."

"Quicksand?"

"Living and dying. That dream scared the shit out of me."

He talks about the night in Vancouver when he and Dill shot up for the first time. They took the miniature train around the Stanley Park animal farm with a bunch of parents and little kids. "You should have seen him, man, he was loving it, the llamas and peacocks, he was so high, I thought he was going to sprout wings."

"All my life," Trudy says, "I've had this feeling. It would be sunny or rainy or windy, I don't know, but I'd get this strong feeling that would bring me close to tears. And then I met Dill and for a while I didn't feel that way anymore."

Kent doesn't speak; he just nods and looks ahead.

"He's on methadone now," she says.

"Here's the difference," Kent says. "You want to know the difference? I'll tell you: I didn't give away my soul."

"He can get it back."

Kent starts the car. "That's what I'm trying to tell you, Trude. He doesn't want it back. No matter what he says, he doesn't want it back."

*

SHE DOESN'T PHONE and neither does Dill. Days go by. She can't eat or sleep or think. At the art gallery where she's taking drawing lessons she slips out to the lobby, but can't bring herself to drop the dime into the payphone, or if she does, she lets it fall through the change slot. Six days after the party, sitting on her bed, she looks out the window at the flat, calm water. The air's so clear you could drink it like vodka. Some kids on a raft are pushing themselves from one beach to another with long poles. Dill lives across the bay and there's the Airstream parked out on the promontory where he used to stand, sending signals with the orange flags he stole from a construction site. *Meet me on the beach. Goodnight. I love you.*

When did he stop sending signals?

It's hot so she takes off her clothes and turns on the electric fan. On top of the bed, air blowing over her body, she thinks about that afternoon at the Bank Street house, the mint julep girl on the porch, her cotton skirt filtering the light. Trudy waited on the ugly orange couch for over an hour, trying to decide — leave or march up the stairs and make a scene? A few guys were watching hockey in the living room, and as she passed the door she heard one of them say, "Who's that?" And then she was at the bottom of the staircase, calling softly as though she didn't really want Dill to hear, calling until his name began to sound like something else. Trudy took off her shoes and tiptoed up the steps, stopping on each one to breathe and slow her heart. At the top, she looked down the narrow hallway, the bright turquoise wainscoting the colour of a swimming pool.

In one of the rooms she found Dill propped up on a bare mattress, his back to the wall. White shirt, loosened tie. Why had he been wearing a shirt and tie? "Hey, Trude," he said when he saw her. A tulip-shaped light fixture hung from the ceiling. The blinds were drawn but a sliver of light shot through a gap, slicing his throat. She crouched beside him and pushed his hair off his face.

"You lied," she said.

"I just wanted to watch. That's the truth, so help me god, and you know it, you know it's the truth, because you're my girl." Kent had nodded off beside him, but Dill kept saying she was his girl, the only girl who'd stick by him through all this bad shit, because let's face it, in a whole lifetime you can count your real friends on one hand. "One hand, Trude, think about it. In your whole life."

"You lied," she said again

"Say it, say you're my girl." He took her hands and squeezed them as though he could wring the words out of her. "Don't be mad. You're so cold when you're mad. You're like my dad when you get like that. I hate that cold shit. Don't do it, Trude."

He took a pen out of his shirt pocket and wrote on the pale underside of her arm: TRUDY LOVES DILL FOREVER. It hurt where he pressed down but she didn't stop him because he was right; she would love him forever. It was her fate to love him. *He* was her fate. He clicked his pen shut in a satisfied way, like a businessman who'd just signed a deal that would give and keep giving. In some frightened part of herself, Trudy accepted all of it. She looked into his eyes, the pupils like tiny imploding black holes, and she saw the truth clearly: she was as wired to Dill as he was to heroin.

*

TWO NIGHTS LATER, she dials his number. Dill's dad answers.

"Dill's sick," he says.

"Sick how?" Trudy says, but she knows.

"Too sick to talk."

"This is Trudy. Will you tell him I called?"

There's no answer. And then Dill's dad hangs up the phone.

The next day she finds a note in the mailbox. A single piece of paper folded inside a hand-delivered envelope, the stamp drawn in the upper right hand corner, a little queen's head, a squiggly crown.

> *Trude:*
> *I used to be a happy little kid but now my spirit is sick. How did this happen?*
> *Dill*

*

SHE WALKS BENEATH trees strung with white lights, hardly aware of what's in front of her — a blur of poplars and azaleas. Dill reads the brochure: *Amaranthus, Cosmos, Dierama, Echinops, Fuchsia, Godetia. . . .* All flowers, all in bloom. In the Rose Garden they stop to kiss beneath an arbour. They kiss in the Japanese Garden leaning against a copper beech. In the Italian Garden they kiss beside a cross-shaped lily pond. The air's redolent with the scent of ten thousand blossoms, and they stop to kiss at every fork in every path because they've been apart for fourteen days and now they're together.

In the centre of what was once an old gravel quarry there's a towering rock garden. Five fountains. The one in the middle shoots water hundreds of feet into the air. At the top of the chiselled stone steps they sit on a bench and when it gets dark and the fireworks begin they share a joint. The sky streaks and flames, brilliant lemon and magenta explosions rain down on their heads, and Trudy can almost imagine a future in which she and Dill graduate from high school, then fly to Europe, leaving all his problems behind.

Hours later, on their way back to the car, he pulls her into the gift shop just as a busload of American tourists enters. There's a frenzy of buying: calendars, tea towels, earthenware pots, postcards, seed packets, gardening tools, bronze gnomes.

Who knew there were so many garden-related things?

"Hey, Trude," Dill says, "what do you want for your birthday?"

Everything. Nothing. That. She points and he reads. "Attractive aluminium watering can with brass insert. Makes a great gift for the gardener on your list."

He's been grinning idiotically since he picked her up earlier and she knows he's high on something more than pot, but she doesn't ask, she doesn't want to know. At the checkout they stand behind a large woman with rings on every finger. After a while Trudy realizes the line isn't moving, that something's wrong, that the woman is hassling the clerk. And then in his ridiculous English accent, Dill is saying, "And what seems to be the problem?" The woman turns to face him, and in a slow aggressive drawl, says, "There's something y'all need to know about us southern gals. We don't take us no damn sass."

Driving back into town, Trudy and Dill laugh. *Y'all need to know. No damn sass.* They laugh until they don't know what they're laughing about, and when the car dips at the end of the avenue, the smell of the sea washes over them and Trudy feels something let go. There's the sensation of falling. Of total body intoxication. Dill drives to his house and parks in the garage. Moving across the back lawn, carrying the watering can, Trudy feels buoyant and fatalistic, as though the sky, made up of a trillion tiny puzzle pieces, is snapping into place. As they pass an open window, she hears the cook singing in Hungarian. The moon is so bright their shadows fall in front of them, and Trudy wonders, Could she turn around now even if she wanted to?

The aerodynamic shell radiates on the promontory, a silver beacon drawing them forward, pulling them inside. In the dark, she and Dill tear at each other, a blind helpless tearing, fumbling with buttons and zippers, and then somehow they're on the floor, somehow they're doing it. No. Dill's doing it. Doing it to her. At her. A stab of pain and she tries to shove him off.

"Hurts," she says.

"Sorry, Trude. Too late now."

And just like that it's over. Just like that he rolls off. She opens her eyes and he's kneeling over her, smiling. Everything has changed and nothing has changed.

"Dill?"

"Hey, Trude, don't be so sad. It's going to be great. You'll see. Now we'll love each other more."

POPE OF ROME

*After the war, rumours spread around the globe: the streets of
Kitimat were paved with gold.* — A Five Year History:
1954- 1959

The wilderness had been carved back to make way for the aluminium smelter, and then carved back some more for the pre-
fab houses in which the men and their families would live. All winter
drifts of snow piled against the front and back doors. Ruby imagined
her father, Johnny Duncan, travelling to and from the smelter in a barrel drum. She imagined him lying inside the drum and rolling along
the roads until he reached his destination. Ruby's mother said Johnny
went to work to make money, so Ruby imagined him standing in front
of a vending machine, pushing buttons. Instead of bags of salty pea-
nuts, coins dropped out.

For breakfast, Ruby and her older sister Nell would sit down to
lumpy porridge and milky tea. On the way out the door their mother
would spoon cod liver oil into their mouths. Once, Ruby found an apple in the fridge, a little stem attached, a leaf attached to that.

"What's this?"

She carried the apple around the house in a doll's blanket. Unwrapped it to show her mother and father. Held it out for her baby sister.

"Look, an apple. A stem. Its own leaf!"

For school photos each child dressed in national costume. That's
Ruby on the front bench — kilt, vest, horrible brogues — face turned
away from the camera, smiling coyly at the boy in lederhosen, sitting
beside her.

Pansies grew in the mounds of earth heaped in half circles in front of
the house. On the new lawn Ruby and Nell lay on either side of their
mother as she flipped through the winter catalogue. Ruby chose a

double-breasted turquoise coat with a lamb's wool collar. A month later when the coat arrived from Vancouver there was something else: a matching pair of snow pants. Ruby hadn't counted on these. These she refused to wear.

*

WHENEVER RAY COOPER came into the house Ruby's mother bristled. Or did she? Maybe she didn't bristle. But she changed somehow, Ruby was sure of that. Maybe it was something in her mother's voice. Ray would bring his accordion in a suitcase lined with crushed velvet. The suitcase was big enough for a small child to sit inside of, so that's what Ruby did. She sat. Bug-eyed bird in a square nest.

"To put some meat on your bones," Ray said to Bette that Saturday night, handing her a black box with gold lettering.

"Poor Ray," Bette said, "can you no find a sweetheart of your own?"

"*You're* my sweetheart," he said, but it was a joke. Ruby knew that. Everyone was his sweetheart, even her.

"Sure there must be a few lassies who'd like a fellow to spoil them," Bette said.

She put the chocolates on the coffee table and told Nell and Ruby to choose one, and one only, and then she went into the kitchen to find some ashtrays.

Ray was a compact swarthy man with a hooked nose and bushy eyebrows. He claimed to believe in three things: progress, keeping an eye open to opportunity, and Ray Cooper. He was snappy, Ruby thought, but not handsome the way her father was handsome, smiling and open-faced with smooth pink skin.

Bette said there were no flies on Ray, but then what did you expect of a Yank?

Nell read the descriptions on the inside of the lid aloud and then both girls chose a chocolate. Ruby sat crossed-legged inside the accordion case and sucked on a hard taffy. She watched the furniture being pushed to the edges of the living room, and then Ray began tapping a foot and playing his accordion. Before long, men were swinging women around, their wide skirts swirling in a dizzying display of floral and checked patterns. No one noticed Ruby slip the chocolate box beneath her sweater and go down the stairs. Sitting on the landing, she began to eat slowly and deliberately, one chocolate after another. She knew she should stop — this was a gift to her mother, after all — but her fingers kept reaching into the little partitions, plucking out malt toffee, carmel finger, hazelnut wafer, coconut eclair.

Later, bent over the toilet, Ruby tried to understand. How had this pleasure — and such pleasure it was — come to this? Between bouts of retching, she raised her head so her mother could wipe her mouth. Nell stood in the doorway, her voice trembling. "How could she?"

Bette seemed to revolve above Ruby's prostrate body, saying things that confused Ruby, left her weak.

The Pope fell down the chapel stairs.

Ruby held her stomach and vomited again.

Nell: "I can't believe it. None left?"

Beads and beads and holy beads, beads and holy water.

Bette held Ruby's hair off her face as she gagged and heaved over the toilet. A long string of saliva hung from her bottom lip.

Hang the Pope and all his folk.

Nell: "She's a greedy little pig."

Ruby wailed, mouth wide, a chute of despair.

*

A MAN FROM the smelter drove to the next town and brought back a truckload of beer. In a few hours every case had sold for double the price. It was before the construction of the *Bear Parlour*, as it came to be known after a bear, drunk on blueberries, stumbled onto the porch and crashed through a window.

That Sunday, Ray and Johnny drank three beers each before coming up with a plan of their own.

"Why not?" Ray said. "Bootlegging's an honourable profession."

Ruby was standing in front of the fridge, rolling back and forth.

"Working for a living," Johnny said, "now *that's* a mug's game."

Snow had been falling for hours and Bette was rinsing diapers at the sink. Bleach fumes rose into the air.

"You're daft, the pair of you," she said. "What sort of man is going to pay three times the cost for a bottle of whiskey? Are they paying you in gold bars at that stinking smelter?"

Ray spread his long, accordion-playing fingers flat on the table. When he laughed his body shook but there was no sound. "Just you wait and see. They'll pay that and more."

Johnny got up and began to roam, looking for the lighter and cigarette package he'd put down minutes before. He kept patting his shirt pocket, as though not convinced. When he strode through the rooms, space seemed to shrink. Rolling back and forth, Ruby became aware of how small the house was with both Ray and her father in it.

"I'll see, will I?" Bette said to Ray. "Have you no conscience? Selling whiskey to men with families to feed."

She wrung out the diapers, piled them in a basin, and went into the living room to hang them over the clotheshorse.

"Not everyone's got a family to feed," Ray called after her. "Some of us have dollar bills burning holes in our pockets."

"You Yanks," Bette called back, "there's no talking to you."

Johnny sat down, his long limbs folding awkwardly into a chair. He flicked his lighter, lit a cigarette, and then reached under the table for two more beers.

"A body needs to let off a little steam now and then," he said, and snapped off a bottle cap. He passed a beer to Ray, and then opened another for himself. They raised their bottles.

"To fortune and friendship," Johnny said.

Ruby pressed her lips against the smooth white surface, and thought: I am kissing the fridge.

*

IT WAS EIGHT in the morning and the baby had been crying for hours. Ruby stood over the hot air vent and looked down at her puffed-out pyjama legs. It was still dark. Snow swirled around the streetlight in front of the house.

"They make me look babyish," she said. "I won't wear them."

"You're not going out that door until you've got them on," Bette said.

Ruby *had* to go out that door. How else would she get to kindergarten, which she loved, which she wished would continue through weekends and summer.

"You're a daft wee fool," Bette said. "I don't know where you get it from." She was swaying back and forth, baby on her hip, rubbing a finger along the baby's gums.

Above the sound of the whistling kettle, Ruby heard the front door close. Nell. As usual, she'd left without complaint, wearing her burgundy coat and matching snow pants, her tartan scarf wound so many times around her head that all you could see were her eyes and tip of her nose.

"I won't. I won't."

Bette put the baby in the playpen, and then went into the kitchen. Ruby followed. In front of the sink she flung herself onto her stomach and pounded the floor with her fists. She thrashed and made loud gasping sounds. She raised her head briefly. Through tears she watched her mother fill the teapot. While the tea steeped, Bette stood by the window and raked her fingers down the steamed-up glass. The baby was still crying. Bette poured a cup of tea, added evaporated milk, and left the kitchen. Ruby turned and smiled grimly at her reflection in the shiny metal cupboards, before half-heartedly going back to kicking and wailing.

From the living room, Bette said, "So help me God, if I have to come in there, I'm going to skelp your backside."

Skelp. Ruby hated that word. *Backside.* That one too. She pulled herself up off the floor and stomped downstairs to her room to get dressed. Back in the kitchen she pulled on her snowpants. Then coat, boots, mitts, scarf. Covered from head to foot, she opened the door but a blast of wind threw her back into the room.

"No one else has to wear them," Ruby shouted. "All the other girls wear leggings."

"I don't care if the Pope of Rome wears leggings," Bette said.

*

RUBY TOOK HER TIME, following in the trenches cut out by kids who'd passed that way earlier. She looked down at her boots, which mutated into small brown animals padding over packed snow. She sang to herself. "*A coo fell offa, a coo fell offa, a coo fell offa a dike. Oooh, a coo fell offa, a coo fell offa a diiiiike.*"

"There you are," Miss Banting said, poking her head into the hall where Ruby was trying to figure out how to get into the cloakroom without being noticed. The teacher directed Ruby into the brightly lit room where the other children were sitting on a braided rug waiting to discuss the weather: snow flurries developing into a snow storm.

"Ruby will be joining us after all," Miss Banting said in such a cheerful voice she might have been announcing that tangerines were falling from the sky. Ruby stood beside her, looking at the unsmiling faces of her classmates. Rolph, the German boy, caught Ruby's eye and smiled. He raised his hand, but in mid-act seemed to decide against waving. It was a funny gesture — the way he pulled his left hand down with his right — and for a moment Ruby forgot her shame.

"Go take off your things," Miss Banting said, and gave Ruby a little push toward the cloakroom. Standing in the corner, Ruby kicked the wall.

Babyish, babyish.

"Are you all right back there?" Miss Banting called.

Later that morning, the teacher asked Ruby to read the instructions on the mimeographed handout. "How to make a snowflake," Ruby read. "Fold a piece of white paper into four parts . . ."

Snowflake, snowstorm, *snow pants.*

I won't, I won't.

"You'll freeze your backside off."

"I hate that word," Ruby'd said to her mother. "Why can't you say something nicer?"

"Nicer?"

"Bottom or rear end."

"Nicer?" Bette repeated, an odd smile on her face. "And what have we here? A right miss, I see."

*

THE WORD WAS OUT. A case of whiskey had arrived the night before. Everyone wanted a bottle. All morning the phone lines hummed with calls for *booze, booze, booze.* Men from the smelter were offering to pay five, eight, twelve bucks.

A week's groceries!

Ironing in front of the window, Bette shook her head. "Daft buggers, the lot of them," she said.

Ruby looked out at Ray's truck idling in the driveway. Johnny was putting on his jacket, pulling a toque down over his head. As he opened the door, Ruby threw her arms around his waist.

"Take me with you."

Bette opened her mouth to protest, then glanced out the window and shrugged. Snow was coming down in blinding sheets.

"It'll be one less wain bouncing off the walls," she said.

Ruby sat in the cab between Ray and her father, watching the windshield wipers move sluggishly back and forth. Ray drove slowly, in the snowplow's wake, to the first address on the list. Johnny got out of the truck and went up to the door, a bottle of whiskey under his arm. A few moments later, Johnny and a little Dutchman with a ruddy face were hollering at Ruby and Ray to come into the house.

Inside, the Dutchman took three glasses out of a cabinet and poured whiskey into each. Sitting on the couch looking around, Ruby was amazed to see that the house was exactly the same as her own, right down to the feature wall, the fake fireplace and the shiny kitchen cupboards. The couch was in a different place, though, and there were pictures on the wall of people standing in fields, windmills behind them. The Dutchman's wife put a plate of open-faced sandwiches on the coffee table. "Eat, eat," she said, then left to attend a crying baby.

Ruby picked a piece of salami off the bread, but before putting it in her mouth, she rolled the salami into a tube and blew through it. She did this several times, stuffing the strange dark bread down the side of a cushion. And then she settled back and listened to the men talk about the smelter and their plans for leaving it. Ray said that once he'd made enough money he was heading south to the big city.

"The women are in Vancouver," the Dutchman said, smiling at Ray. "No women up here."

"And at the rate they're reproducing," he said, reaching over and messing up Ruby's bowl cut, "it's no wonder the newspapers are predicting — what is it? —a population explosion."

Johnny said he was thinking of emigrating to the States, Oregon or California. He wanted to buy an orange orchard, run his own show.

This was news to Ruby.

"I don't want to leave Kitimat," she said. "It's the most beautiful city in the world."

Her father slapped his knee and laughed. Other people always joined in when Johnny laughed. "The most beautiful city," he said. "How do you like that? This hell hole."

And all three men laughed again.

The Dutchman offered Ray and Johnny another glass of whiskey but Johnny said, Thanks just the same, they had to get going.

At the next house, a few streets over, Ruby, Johnny and Ray all walked up to the front door and rang the bell.

"Gino," Ray said to a sullen-looking man with tight curly hair, "look what we brought you. An early Christmas present."

Gino grasped the whiskey bottle by the neck and held it up like a trophy. With his other fist he thumped his chest as though dislodging a piece of gristle. "*Molto grazie*," he said, then he too poured drinks for everyone, including his pregnant wife who kept smiling and pointing at Ruby and then smiling and pointing at Johnny.

The adults talked and smoked and drank while Ruby looked around, observing the identical floor plan but different furnishings and knick-knacks. Bored, she picked up the bottle on the table and swirled the liquid around. *Distilled Blended and Bottled in Scotland.* On the label was a little man in white trousers, black boots, a red jacket with tails. Ruby could imagine her mother saying, "Doesn't he fancy himself?"

Johnny finished his whiskey and looked at his daughter. "Give us a wee song, there's a good lass."

Gino's wife clapped her hands: "Yes, yes, a song."

Ruby got up and stood in front of the adults and began to sing softly. *Just a wee doch-an-doris, just a wee dram that's a, just a wee doch-an-doris before we gang a-wa, there's a wee wifie waitin', in a wee butt an ben . . .*

What did this mean? Ruby watched Johnny's flushed face as the strange words flowed from her mouth. He looked so proud that she kept going and by the end she was shouting out the lyrics. *If you can say, "It's a braw bricht moonlicht nicht" ye a'richt ye ken.*

The adults clapped and laughed and Ruby looked down at her feet.

"It's been a real pleasure," Ray said, "but there's a few more waiting for the milkman's deliveries."

In the kitchen, putting on her coat and boots, Ruby could hear Gino and his wife in the next room talking excitedly to each other in Italian. They seemed to have forgotten their guests. Johnny shrugged and smiled. "That's Mr. Walker for you."

Outside, Ruby stood beside the truck, fat snowflakes melting on her face, and looked back at the house. Gino and his wife were leaning out a window and waving.

"*Arrividerci. Arrividerci.*"

Next, Ray drove to the house of an Irishman with two boys. Inside, it looked nothing like the others. The living room was a disaster: deep gouges in the gyprock, black tarpaper covering a hole in the window, a vacuum cleaner in pieces, women's shoes, a pie plate full of cigarette butts, pots and pans, clothes and dishes strewn everywhere. Other than a few kitchen chairs there was almost no furniture.

The Irishman poured whiskies for all three men and began to talk about his wife, who, it seemed, had gone back to Dublin because a Polish doctor had said she was heading for a nervous breakdown.

"Bloody foreigner," the Irishman said.

Ruby watched his sons slap a puck back and forth between the men's legs, from one corner of the room to the other. Every now and then one of the boys would shout, "Geronimo."

The Irishman said he had an awful feeling his wife was not coming back. It was right depressing, so it was.

When the boys tired of hockey, they offered to show Ruby their bedroom. It was identical to hers and Nell's, except that the boys, using wax crayons, had scribbled on all fours walls, from floor to ceiling, moving their bunk beds around the room as a kind of scaffolding.

For the rest of the afternoon Ray and Johnny and Ruby went from one house to another, delivering bottles of whiskey. At each residence the men smoked and drank and talked about their plans for leaving Kitimat. As the afternoon progressed Ray became quiet and Johnny's future plans became more grandiose. Now he was talking about buying up real estate in Texas.

"Land," he kept saying, "that's where the money is."

It was dark when the truck slowly wound its way back through the snow-clogged streets. When it fishtailed on ice and Ray swerved into a ditch, they got out of the driver's side and walked the rest of the way home. Ruby ran circles around her father as he slipped and slid along the street, laughing and congratulating them all on the day's success.

Bette opened the door. "You're half cut," she said.

"Not at all," Johnny said. "We're entrepreneurs." He leaned against the doorframe as though to ponder a thought. "Entrepreneur. That's a difficult word to say."

"You're half cut," Bette said again.

Ruby hung her coat on a hook and then sat at the table beside Nell. In her highchair, the baby was kicking her feet and leaning forward, crying for her metal bowl, which had flipped upside down onto the floor. A dough ball lay beside it.

"You'll be glad to hear we made a decent profit," Ray said to Bette. "Enough to invest in three more cases. And that's not counting the bottle we kept for ourselves."

"Now then," Johnny said, "I forgot about the bottle we kept for ourselves. Shall we treat ourselves to a nip before supper?"

Bette put plates of stew on the table and told the men to sit down and eat. She asked how Ray was going to drive home in his condition.

Reaching clumsily for his wife, Johnny said, "Will you no join us for a wee drap?"

"John Andrew Duncan, I wouldn't join you for a wee drap if you were the Pope of Rome."

"I thought the Scots were fond of their whiskey," Ray said. "You've disappointed me, sweetheart. You really have."

Johnny said he felt a little worse for wear and he went to the bedroom and lay on the floor. Bette brought sheets and blankets out to the living room and made up a bed on the couch for Ray. Later, unable to sleep, Ruby got up to go to the bathroom. On her way up the stairs, she heard Ray and her mother talking.

"Are you daft, man?"

Ruby's feet were cold and she had to pee, but she stood and listened.

"The girls come too," Ray said. "Whatever you want. Just think about it, that's all I'm saying, give it some thought, will you do that at least?

Bette laughed.

"I'm not leaving without you," Ray said.

"You will leave."

Ray sighed.

"Can you no see what's in front of your eyes?" Bette said.

And then she began to talk about the endless winter, how it went on and on and on with no end in sight. "It was enough to drive anyone bammy," she said. "Look at the way poor Gallager O'Brian went round the bend."

"Take it easy," Ray said, "take it easy, sweetheart."

With this, Ruby stood bolt upright and marched noisily up the stairs. When she got to the top she didn't look in her mother and Ray's direction but kept walking.

"Who's there?" Bette said. She followed Ruby into the bathroom and stood over her, arms crossed, watching her daughter's face as she sat on the toilet. "Ray's drunk," Bette said. "You know that don't you? He's no idea what he's talking about."

Ruby pulled up her pyjama bottoms and flushed the toilet and then she leaned over the sink for a drink from the tap.

"That's the way men get with whiskey," her mother continued. "They say daft things."

Ruby looked out the window at the icicles hanging from the eves and thought, I could ask her for anything right now, anything in the world.

"It's freezing downstairs," she said. "I want the water bottle."

For a moment, Bette stared hard at her daughter, as though trying to decide. "I'll bring it down," she said. "Now off you go, there's a good hen."

The next morning the sheets and blankets were folded at the end of the couch and Ray was gone. Johnny hadn't gotten up for work and when Ruby finished breakfast he was still in bed. She asked what was the matter and Bette said, "Your father had a bad case of the blarney yesterday and is now suffering for it like the fool he is."

Nell said he had a hangover.

Ruby went into her parent's dark bedroom and stood beside her sleeping father. She didn't know what a hangover was but she'd expected something else. She'd expected to find him standing in the clothes closet, his head, not in stocks, but caught nevertheless — stuck in a coat-hanger. Johnny didn't open his eyes but he must have known she was there, because, barely moving his lips, he said, "What did you make of our day in the bootlegging business?"

Ruby placed her hand on her father's forehead. It was cool and damp. "Good," she said.

*

SPRING FINALLY ARRIVED. Ruby and her friend, Dierdre, liked to walk to the library, a low flat bunker, and take out three books each. On the way home they'd kneel on the wooden sidewalk and try to fish out coins that had fallen into the snow over winter. That day Ruby found a nickel. Now Deirdre was leaning forward, hands placed on her slightly bent knees. She began to speak to Ruby as though she were a child. They were both five. Ruby stepped back and glanced down: black mud on either side of the sidewalk. She could hear a river, ice breaking up, water running loose.

Deirdre was speaking patiently. "You want to be fair don't you?"

Earlier, in the library washroom, they'd washed their hands with pink soap from the dispenser above the sink. Deirdre had also scrubbed her face and even rolled up her sleeves to rub the soap on her arms. Now her cheeks were blotchy.

"Give it to me," she said, "or I won't be your friend."

Ruby stared into Deirdre's eyes — pale blue with yellow rims — and thought, She is blocking out all my light. She always blocks out my light. Ruby realized that whenever she and Deirdre played together, it ended badly, in blows and tears. But never this: I won't be your friend.

The smell of fresh earth bloomed in Ruby's head as she reached into her pocket. Deirdre's tongue was moving over chapped lips. Ruby handed her the coin. Without a word, Deirdre turned and started walking away, back to the crescent-shaped streets named after birds — Sterling, Quail, Wren, Partridge.

Ruby thought: There goes my nickel.

Everywhere bulldozers were pushing up gravel. Freshly cut lumber was being hoisted and laid across beams. The rhythm of power saws, the din of pounding hammers, men throwing off their jackets and calling to each other in twenty-five languages. Standing on the sidewalk, between the library and the Hudson's Bay Post, Ruby felt the sun's warmth radiate through her body. She unzipped the reindeer sweater her mother had knit using fat needles and stepped down from the wooden planks. Mud oozed up and over the tops of her boots. She waited, holding her breath, while the cold squishy blackness penetrated the spaces between her toes. And then she kneeled, plunging her hands into the mud. It was sickening and thrilling, like burying something alive.

*

THE THEATRE OPENED to fanfare and celebration. There was a May Day parade with three marching bands, a clown who threw candies into the crowd, and a float from which the first Alcan Beauty Queen waved her long-gloved hand. Ruby was wearing the bonnet she wore to the Presbyterian Church on Easter Sunday. The ribbons made her chin itch. Inside the theatre, kids were running in the aisles. They were shouting and jumping on the seats, flipping them up and down. Ruby and Nell sat close to the front and immediately the girl beside Ruby spilled Coca-Cola on Ruby's shoe.

Popcorn zinged above her head.

When the lights went down, the silence was so utter that Ruby clutched the arms of her seat. And then the beam of light above her head, the film unrolling, its rhythmic *tick, tick, tick.* Though she tried to concentrate, she couldn't follow the plot. In baffling succession one awful image after another flashed before her: a man beating a boy, the blood of a pig, a dead man in a riverboat. There were rainstorms and murders, a small raft bucking in waves. The movie seemed to roll on for hours and hours. Surely days have passed, Ruby thought, as confusion piled upon confusion, and a black-skinned man ran through fields and woods. Ruby had never seen a Negro before. The enormous whites of his eyes were terrified and terrifying. The theatre exploded with gunfire and dogs' barking. Boots crashed through the underbrush, and then the Negro's feet filled the screen. Huge dark bleeding feet with pink soles scrabbled over fallen logs and splashed through creek beds, the music rising to an unbearable pitch.

Ruby began to bawl.

Nell jabbed her sister but Ruby only bawled louder. She kept bawling as kids all around booed and threw crumpled bags at her head. *Shut up, cry baby.* She bawled until the end of the movie, and she was still bawling when Johnny and Ray drove up to the theatre in Johnny's new green Pontiac with the Indianhead hood ornament. Ray jumped out of the passenger's side and crouched on the sidewalk. He stunk of beer and tobacco and his tongue was playing with the toothpick in his mouth.

"What's the matter, sweetheart?"

The wind was blowing and Ruby could feel tears welling in her eyes as she tried to hold her skirt flat against her legs. She looked at Ray and thought, Why is he always here? With the heel of her hand, she pushed hard against his forehead.

"Go," she said. "Go away."

"Hey, what's got your goat?" he said. He looked at Nell, standing by the car. "What's got her goat?"

"I'm not going anywhere with her again," Nell said.

They all got in the car and as Johnny pulled away from the theatre he looked in the rear view mirror at Ruby's face.

"I thought that was supposed to be a picture for wains," he said to Ray, but before Ray could answer, Nell leaned forward and angrily repeated herself, "I am never *ever* going anywhere with her again."

Ruby lay her head against the vibrating car window which caused the sounds coming out of her mouth to waver in an interesting way. She bawled all the way to Swallow Street and was still bawling as she got out of the car and walked ahead of her sister and father and Ray, up the front steps and into the house.

*

JOHNNY PARKED at a distance from the mountains of garbage. Ruby and Nell fought each other to be first out of the car and up on the front hood. Fireweed had sprung up in the open spaces, tall purple spikes that smelled of sweetness and death. Bette rolled down the window but stayed inside. Johnny got out of the car and reached for the baby. Earlier, over dinner, he'd said, "I should have seen it coming, Ray wasn't cut out for the smelter."

"Some men think they're too good," Bette said.

Ruby thought of the little dapper man on the whiskey bottle. She imagined Ray walking down the street, swinging a stick and tipping his top hat.

"It's a shame," Johnny said. "If he'd stayed, he'd have made foreman in another six months time."

"Don't worry about Ray," Bette said, "he'll do all right for himself."

Johnny chewed slowly on his meat, then swallowed and took a drink of water.

"It's just as well," he said.

Bette put down her fork. "What do you mean by that?"

Johnny stabbed another piece of meat.

"I mean what I said. It's just as well."

Ruby scanned the edge of the dump, where the forest began, dense and unrelenting. Cedars, hemlock, Sitka spruce. It was late June and the sky was luminescent. And then she saw them coming out of the trees: three bears, one large and two small. The biggest one lumbered forward, head turning this way and that. It got up on its hind legs and began to forage through the garbage like a woman at a church bizarre, picking things up and dropping them.

The baby began to squirm in Johnny's arms.

"Whisht," Johnny whispered. "They're wild animals, we don't want them to know we're here."

But they did know.

Three dark heads swung round, and for a long moment one family stared at another. And then, unable to contain herself, Ruby stabbed the air with a finger.

"Look. There. Over there!"

She glanced back at the windshield, expecting to see her mother's eyes lit up with excitement. Instead, Bette's stricken face peered back at her from the other side of the glass.

HITCHHIKE

Jayne, long-legged and fifteen, spells her name with a Y and hitch-hikes to school. At eight o'clock there's always a steady flow of traffic moving past her house. It's so easy. She just steps outside and sticks out her thumb. A few minutes of standing in the rain and she's climbing into a warm plush car. The radio's playing light rock. The drive to her high school takes approximately twenty minutes. For the duration she asks the driver about his job/hobbies/wife/children. She says *his* but on the rare occasion, and she means rare, a woman picks her up.

People like to talk. About themselves mainly but about other things too. And Jayne is genuinely interested. She believes every story is fasci-nating, every person has a story to tell. And she has a way of drawing them out. For a brief time the driver forgets he's forty and balding, for-gets it's Tuesday morning and he's going to spend much of his life in an airless cubicle, drinking bad coffee. Last night his daughter ate all the play-dough and wet her bed, but these details dissipate in the blast of damp air Jayne brings in from outside. Suddenly there she is in her high boots and lip gloss, asking *who what why.*

She wants to know everything. Even so, her questions veer away from the big subjects: religion, politics, sex. Especially sex. These, after all, are things about which Jayne knows little. She may lack the corset and Gibson Girl hairdo but like a Victorian woman she's most com-fortable engaging in light conversation. She could be holding a china teacup, watching a game of lawn tennis. She could be juggling balls in the air. To bring up sickness and death, for instance, more specifically, death by colon cancer, would be to watch the balls plummet, to hear the thud as they land on the grass.

If asked, she'd have to say men are easier to talk to. Men, it seems, are willing to believe she has momentarily fallen in love with them.

Women are suspicious. Of what Jayne's not sure. Though she suspects. She has a sister and knows what girls want. And what they want, they want from each other.

Jayne wants a ride.

And she believes each journey, no matter how insignificant, should be at least tolerably pleasant. Life is too short to waste on unpleasantness. Where she's heard this she doesn't know, though she guesses it's from her mother. She guesses her mother has said on more than one occasion it is best to speak agreeably about agreeable things.

Jayne develops regulars. There's the man who picks her up several days a week in a red Porsche and looks like Brad Pitt, no kidding, he looks like Brad Pitt. Which doesn't particularly impress Jayne. She has a thing for Tom Cruise. Ever since *Rainman*, his cobalt eyes.

She doesn't know the names of any of her drivers. It's not something she asks. And she never offers her own. Anonymity is part of the unspoken twenty minute contract. At least that's how Jayne sees it. Ideally, she'd like dotted lines on which both she and the driver could scribble their signatures before slipping into gear and heading down the road. She believes a signature tells a lot. She believes a person's cursive script reveals the soul.

Jayne asks the Porsche guy about his job, and he tells her he works in finance. He knows her friend's oldest sister who is also a stockbroker, so he's not a liar. Though he is definitely trying to impress. Jayne's heard the saying *money talks* but when he starts to talk about money she looks out the window.

It's obvious this man is pleased with himself. In his designer suit and expensive cologne, he is extremely pleased. No doubt he imagines he's doing Jayne a favour. But she sees it differently. He's in his thirties and still in love with the woman in his bed. He's in love with all the women in his bed. The way he looks at Jayne when he asks what she'd like to listen to — Bob Marley or Annie Difranco? — makes her knees tremble slightly beneath her textbooks, and she wonders if she'd like to be one of those women.

It's Monday morning and half way to school he puts on Emmy Lou Harris' "The Wrecking Ball," a gift from his mother.

Emmy's singing "Sweet Old World" as Jayne gets out of the

Porsche and waves over her shoulder. Thanks for the ride. See ya. Inside the school she walks to her locker, and then to her first class, on the edge of something, hearing Emmy's words play in her mind. She keeps getting this weird feeling that she's about to pitch forward into blackness, a blackness so huge and deep she'll never be able to crawl back out.

Jayne doesn't pry. It isn't necessary. What she learns at fifteen: if you listen, people will talk. She is a grief counsellor in the making. Though she wants to be a graphologist. She wants to work for the RCMP and decipher the handwriting of criminals and deviants. She imagines herself a kind of detective, undercover, with an expense account and a first class ticket to Moscow. Toward this end she has taken out books from the city library: *Graphology: A Practical Course in Fifteen Lessons* and *Handwriting: A Key to Personality.*

Jayne asks her friends to bring samples from home. When Rowan offers a grocery list she says, Your mother is resilient and emotionally stable but has poor organizational skills. The letter from Sarah's grandfather reveals the old man is dependable and has a good social attitude. "But look here," Jayne says, "the consistent back-slant indicates fear." Fear of what? Sarah wants to know but Jayne can only guess. "Fear of life," she says, "fear of death."

Jayne mentions her interest in graphology to a woman who gives her a ride. She mentions her plan to turn this interest into a career. The woman, not one of Jayne's regulars, laughs and says, "Is that the best thing you can think of doing with your life?" She's a white-knuckle driver who grips the steering wheel as though she's avoiding mine fields and driving through road blocks. The woman's response surprises Jayne. For the past year she's assumed that interpreting the aberrant mind through forged cheques and ransom notes is as interesting as it gets.

"You've got to be joking," the woman says. "That's palm reading. That's crystal balls."

But no, Jayne insists, graphology is a science, it's based on empirical evidence.

The woman laughs again, this time trillingly. "Hocus-pocus," she says. "Here's your stop."

A man in a baseball cap stops for Jayne. Within minutes she learns he was a fighter pilot in the first Gulf War. Jayne prides herself on how quickly she can hone in on a life. It's like skating through a line of defence and slipping the puck into the net. "That must've been scary," she says. She knows it's a clichéd thing to say even as she says it, but the pilot doesn't seem to care. After all, he expects such words to come out of her mouth. She's only a girl and he's a man who's seen it all. His body tenses just to remember those night flights over Jordon. Why, in the years since, he hasn't experienced anything like it. "The camaraderie alone," he says, turning to Jayne, a girl sipping from a water bottle in the seat beside him.

She is sincere. The twenty minute ride to school is the best part of her day. After that, it goes downhill, and she means fast. Biology, French, Algebra. Nothing's as good as her morning encounter. Though she likes to think of it as a fair exchange: she gets a free ride and the driver gets to reminisce. In the pilot's case, about dropping bombs on Iraqis.

"Best time of my life," he says, looking over, assuming she understands, at least this much. But Jayne doesn't understand. Quite frankly, she doesn't get it at all. She's against killing. Why else would she have become a vegetarian? Though she doesn't tell the fighter pilot this. She doesn't tell him even her father, lover of barbecued ribs, finally stopped eating meat because of the toxins. She doesn't want to break the flow. The conversation is going so well.

It's June and the oak trees lining the streets have unfurled their green. All her exams are behind her or about to be written. The longest day of the year is so close she can smell the light. It's sandals and halter top weather the morning Jayne sticks out her thumb, stopping a white Echo. She pops her head in to ask if the man's going as far as her school. He nods and she slides into the seat. The artsy type, she thinks, glancing over. Linen trousers, glasses, brown loafers without socks. But this one doesn't respond to her questions (So how's it going? Think it's gonna rain?), and when she stops talking he doesn't speak. Jayne tries to think of topics, things of general interest, but all that comes to mind is the Buddhist she heard on the radio the night before, saying he survived bone cancer because his Zen friends chanted at his bedside around the clock. "I wanted to die," the Buddhist said, "it would have been so much easier, but my Sensai kept calling me back." Jayne knows this Zen thing is not exactly an ice-breaker so she doesn't bring it up.

Twenty minutes of uninterrupted silence.

As the Echo approaches her corner, she says, "Here. This is good, stop here." The man shifts down but the car keeps rolling. Past the intersection. Past the wood chip island where mothers push their children on swings. The car's going so slowly now she has time to wonder about a girl not much older than herself. The ponytail on top of her head has slipped to the side. She looks off-kilter. Jayne cocks her head to put the girl right. And the expression on her face — desperate or exultant as she kneels at the bottom of the slide, arms wide to catch the child?

"Stop," Jayne says again. "Here." The driver takes his foot off the gas pedal. Out the corner of her eye she can see he's pulled down his zipper, that he's rubbing something in his lap. She can guess what it is. The world slurs past the car window — a man walking a white poodle, another rollerblading in shorts, his simmering strides. Telephone poles, oak trees, their unfurled green.

Jayne looks down at the library book in her lap: *Handwriting Analysis: The Complete Basic Program* and wonders if it holds the answer to her problem, the problem inside this fuel-efficient car, a car that won't stop? She stares at the book's cover remembering that it's five days overdue, that she doesn't want to return it, she wants to go through it one more time, this book with chapters on everything she needs to know about zones, pressure, spacing, rhythm, connectedness and disconnectedness.

With great effort, Jayne's brain sends a message to her arm: Lift the handle. She pushes against the passenger door and while the car is still moving jumps onto the boulevard. Pens and books fly. A ridiculous exit. On hands and knees, she looks up as the Echo's license plate slips out of sight.

After Math, Jayne walks down the hall with a boy who sits at the back of the room. She has been observing him all year. He holds out a bag of salt and vinegar potato chips and nods, inviting her to take some. While they walk, she tells him about the guy who gave her a ride; she tells him about the silence and zipper and how it was all pretty lame and then she can't go on.

"Fucking perv," the boy says.

Jayne's mouth is dry. The potato chips wad up and become difficult to swallow.

Standing in front of the boy's locker, looking at his hemp necklace, the small beads woven into the pattern, she notices his eyes. The word turquoise comes to mind. The south of France comes to mind. The summer before her father was diagnosed with cancer. In a rented Megane he drove the coast road while in the back seat she and her sister went blind looking out at the Mediterranean.

"The Côte d'Azure," Jayne says. And then liking the sound she says it again. Azure, azure. She writes the word across the boy's forehead in large looping letters. He gives her a look. He gives her such a look that she thinks she could talk to this boy, she could describe the size and slant and depth of her regret. The afternoon sun is a column of light pouring through the arched window at the end of the hallway, and she thinks she could tell this boy that she wishes she'd chanted at her father's bedside, she wishes she'd chanted and sung and prayed day and night, she wishes she'd pressed her mouth to his ear and begged him not to give up, to please please hold on.

To this world, this sweet old world.

Yes, Jayne thinks, to this boy, she could say anything.

NO GIZMOS

Thirty bucks," I say, "it's my last offer." It's nine, already hot. Dina's on my hip, big eyes swivelling. "See for yourself, it's a compact house." With my free hand I make a flourishing gesture. He leans against a post, rubbing his chin. I can feel the stubble, the lousy itch of it. "Nobody's getting rich in these small town pageants," he says, and I slide a foot across the porch, tip Butchy's GI Joe truck down the steps. Ka-klunk, ka-klunk. I smile my I've-got-all-the-time-in-the-world smile. He smirks his low-life romantic smirk. We both watch a rubber wheel wobble across the driveway.

*

Fast Eddy, she's fast, whipping around the yard, sprinkling water from a plastic watering can. The bedding plants I put in last week are covered in little yellow flowers.

"Have a drink," she says to each one. "No, really, it's on me."

We're best friends, Eddy and me. She says it's because we live in the same house, that we'll break apart when I move out, move on, figure out where I'm going, but I say, no, I say I'd prefer her company any time, anywhere.

We drink liquorice tea in the gazebo. Morning glory spits white trumpets through squares of lattice. Fast Eddy's kid is running back and forth through the sprinkler. Butchy's an eight year old Sumo wrestler, a mass of jiggling blubber. Dina stands back, mesmerized. The druggy scent of honeysuckle and lilac muddies my brain but not Fast Eddy's. She's onto something revolutionary: healing pain.

Standing behind me, she's making these quick movements above my head. Her hands swoop down, as though describing a teepee. She flicks her fingers above a bucket of salt. Her breath synchronizes with

117

her movements and everything slows — Butchy lumbering across the lawn, Dina crawling over the grass, the sprinkler throwing out delicate whips of water.

*

The windows aren't dirty; he washed them last week and the week before that. In fact, they're so squeaky clean you can't tell there's glass inside the frames. Some people don't care if their windows are covered in bird shit and grime. They don't care if the sun's shining or it's pouring rain. I used to be one of those people. It was okay by me if I never saw the light of day. I had other things on my mind.

But that all changed when the window washer turned up, knocking on doors, looking for business.

I walk into the bedroom and act surprised. I wave as though I just happen to be passing through. Hey, I am just passing through. I reach for a pillow, plump it, throw it back on the bed. For a brief moment, so brief I don't know if it's real, he stops what he's doing, right there on the ladder, and plays a few licks on the air guitar. He doesn't actually sing but I hear something just the same.

"I'm gonna get you down to twenty bucks," I say. "Gonna get you down." He laughs. Raucous, sentimental. A nuts and bolts kind of laugh. "Cash," I say. "Under the table."

*

Fast Eddy's a cocktail waitress, full time, big tips. She says, "All you gotta do is shake your booty." I babysit Butchy in exchange for rent. It's a good arrangement except for the fact that he's one messed up kid. When Social Services delivered him to 3135 Albert Street eight months ago his clothes stank. They still stink. All the hot water and heavy duty detergent in the world can't wash out that stink.

Fast Eddy blames herself for what happened out on the mink farm. It was irresponsible of her to dump Butchy on her ex, but, she says, "I'm not the maternal type. Not like you, Syl. You're a fucking earth mother."

This morning another pissed-off woman stomped up the front steps, hauling her boy by the arm.

"Look what your kid did to my kid."

Not my kid, I thought, never has been, never will be.

Last week a black eye, the week before that, a dislocated shoulder.

"Butchy doesn't know his own strength," I told the woman. "He lives full tilt, burns up more energy than Montreal."

*

THE WINDOW WASHER's looking up at me through the big picture window. Tight jeans, a torn shirt. He's bow-legged, wearing ass-kicking cowboy boots. He capers around Eddy's fiberglass boat like it's not even there. Some window washers use a long pole with a brush at the end but not this one. Just a bucket and a rag. The basics. No gizmos. He steps onto the ladder and Dina and I watch his ascent, one rung at a time.

"Light," she whispers, holding up a hand.

When he's eye level, I lock on, feel my ribcage blow slowly apart.

*

FAST EDDY TUCKS her hair behind her ears and then picks up the pad and pen on the table between us. She purses her lips and I tell her there's this stranger who needs a place to stay for the night, so I offer him the couch. I look across the lawn where Dina's holding the end of the hose. It's gurgling water. She brings the nozzle to her mouth, and then pulls back in fright.

Fast Eddy says, "The dream, Syl, concentrate."

"The guy's a total sleaze and Dina's a newborn again. She's always a newborn, you noticed that?"

"Definitely a recurring pattern," Fast Eddy says.

"So, she's in her crib, soaked through, and the guy starts roaming around. 'I'm hungry,' he whines. 'I wanna watch hockey.' A real moron. I change Dina's diaper and undershirt, put her in a clean sleeper. I do all this, you know, methodically, like I'm wrapping a package to send to the North Pole or something. And then I'm on a train heading for a crappy beach resort."

Fast Eddy writes down *sleeper, train, beach resort.*

"That's when I remember Dina's alone in the house with the creep."

"Probably lasted ten seconds," Fast Eddy says. "In real time, I mean."

"But here's the thing," I say. "You're on the train too. And you say, 'A stone,' get this, 'a stone would solve everything.'"

*

OLD MAN O'RILEY phoned the cops but when they came to look into the problem of Fast Eddy's eighteen-foot boat parked on the street, he was so hammered he started shouting, "Get the hell off my property or I'll call the cops!"

After the third ticket Fast Eddy tore down the fence and had the boat pulled up onto the lawn.

The youngest O'Riley boy reminds me of that cartoon character, Rocket J. Squirrel. Fast Eddy says he's a genius. The older one's good looking enough, with sad dark eyes, but too feminine for my taste. Across the street, there's a family of Bible thumpers. The Sikh family doesn't mix either. They walk out in the evening altogether, the turbaned father in front, the mother and girls following behind in beautiful colours. Maybe they've been walking out in the evenings for years. How would I know? I've just begun to notice life on Albert Street. My eyes snapped open around the time the window washer appeared on the scene, kicking up the pavement, and purring *sha na na.*

*

"MY DAD SAYS Fast Eddy's getting ready for the flood," the Bible thumpers' kid says. He's hitting the tetherball in the backyard and I'm on the deck above, spreading Dina's clean clothes over the plastic chairs to dry.

Butchy says, "What're you talking about?"

The kid keeps leaping into the air, flailing his fists at the ball as it passes above his head. "My dad says Fast Eddy's going to float away with all the animals."

"What animals?" Butchy says. "There's no animals."

"Fast Eddy's a queer lesbo," the kid says.

"You're a lesbo," Butchy says.

"My dad says Fast Eddy must think it's gonna rain forty days and forty nights."

Butchy grips the metal pole with both hands and starts to shake.

"Hey, quit doing that, I'm trying to . . ."

Someone swats someone and by the time I get down the stairs the kid's wailing his eyes out.

*

"Spectacular," Fast Eddy says, strolling around the deck. "How do you do it, Syl?"

She means how do I grow these terrific tomatoes.

There are days when Fast Eddy thinks everything is spectacular and today is one of them. Some nights when I come out here to kneel among the terra cotta pots, a river runs through me.

Eddy plucks off a few suckers.

"Spectacular," she says again. "Truly spectacular."

*

Normally i wouldn't buy bedding from Sally Anne's but these pillowcases were impressive. Like finding diamonds in a barrel of scraps. Sure, they're worn, but they're made out of some kind of velvety, high-thread count cotton. I put a couple on Fast Eddy's pillows and my guess is she slept like a baby.

"Who the hell is J. L. Rutledge?" she says this morning.

"How should I know?"

"Where'd those pillowcases come from?"

"Who cares? They're white, they're clean."

Butchy's watching TV in the living room — goons in caveman outfits smashing chairs over each other's skulls and Fast Eddy's pouring herself another cup of coffee. Her shift starts at ten. I wish she'd get moving. The Social Worker's coming later and already I'm so nervous I can only speak in monosyllables.

"Those pillowcases must've come from a rest home," Fast Eddy says. "They write names on stuff so it doesn't get mixed up."

"What if they do?"

"I could've been lying on some old guy's pillowcase. Christ, some dead old geezer."

*

"NICE DAY," I say, leaning over the deck railing. The window washer looks up and squints.

"The rush of the moment," he says. "That's what we live for."

A bandana holds the hair out of his eyes. He's tightly muscled, a wound-up pin-ball machine. And then, I hear her before I see her — the Bible thumper, like an Arctic wind funnelling down the north side of the house.

"If I get my hands on that kid, so help me God."

She turns the corner, glances around the yard, then up at me.

"Beefsteak," I say to the window washer. "Catch."

He holds out his hands.

"Who're you talking to?" the woman says.

The window washer bites into the tomato, seeds spurting every-where. He wipes his mouth with the back of his hand.

The Bible thumper turns around and around, confused. "I'd like to talk to the boy's mother."

I take one last look at him, torso swivelling on ball bearings, then turn and walk away.

*

SOME ANIMAL liberation types stole onto Fast Eddy's ex's farm and took wire clippers to the cages. They freed five hundred mink. When the cops arrived to cover the crime they observed Butchy's dismal situation for themselves. Which led to Social Services becoming involved.

Which led to Fast Eddy gaining sole custody. Which led to me being assessed a qualified childminder. Turns out the liberated mink scattered into the nearby Forest Owl Sanctuary where they set about killing birds about to be released back into the wild.

"Now there's irony for you," Fast Eddy said. "If you're looking for a definition of irony, that would be it."

*

DINA STANDS in her little blow up pool on the deck, patting the ruffly bottom of her underpants. "Nudey Puss," Butchy says. He doesn't know I'm watching through the window above the sink. He shoves her in the chest. She falls backwards, sits in two inches of water, stunned. I knock hard on the glass, like I'm going to clobber him. Like I'm *really* going to clobber him.

*

THE O'RILEYS drive past. The genius waves. I wave back, like I'm a beauty queen on a May Day float.

Fast Eddy says, "Everyone wants something. What do you want?"

We do this on her nights off, sit inside the wheel house and drink beer.

I shrug.

"A man?" she says. "Do you want a man?"

"No man," I say.

"A woman?" Fast Eddy says.

"No woman," I say. "Not even a good one."

Fast Eddy laughs.

"You ever think of putting this boat in the water?" I say.

"The things you come up with," she says.

It has an inboard motor, a flying bridge and a small galley with everything you can think of, even little plastic corn cob holders in the shape of little plastic corn cobs. Sitting on Fast Eddy's lap, Dina steers the steering wheel and I think, she's good to my baby, she's trying her best with her fucked-up excuse-for-a-kid. Me, I don't know how much longer I can do it. It's not as though the social worker didn't warn me.

Fast Eddy's ex and his girlfriend used to lock Butchy in his room, then go out to the bar. Sometimes they left food, sometimes they didn't. Sometimes they left the light on, sometimes they didn't.

"This child is a tragic case of neglect," the social worker told me. "When he starts to act out, stop and think."

Fast Eddy says the fucking mink got better treatment.

I don't tell her I *do* want something. I don't tell her that sometimes I get so crazy with wanting, pieces of me splinter and fly off in all directions.

The sun dips behind the house. On the other side of the street the Sikh family lands on the sidewalk like a flock of brilliant birds. I twist round to pull on my cardigan and that's when I see Butchy at the window. Stubby hands on glass, webbed fingers. How long has he been standing there, watching?

*

I throw Dina's rag doll in the air, grab its hand on the way down. The window washer is on the ladder leaning against the house. "You gotta know where you're coming from," he says. "Where you're headed."

This is what he tells me. He tells me such things.

Nothing between us now but a pane of glass. I toss the doll into Dina's crib, scrunch one of J. L. Rutledge's pillowcases in my fist and start wiping down the inside, the mucky fingerprints and drooling mouth marks.

"Ready for a carnival ride?" he says, and the window washer and I, we get a rhythm thing going, grinding down with it, belly against belly. I drop the pillowcase and spread my arms. Press my body against the window. This is what it feels like to rush toward your destiny, to meet it head on. I close my eyes, feel my lips go soft, and when I open them, he's gone.

I'm alone in Dina's room, staring at the metal pole in the yard, the ball dangling at the end of its tether.

Silence like I've never heard.

The sun's directly overhead; heat's rising in yellow waves. I hear scuttling, yelps, a crash? I don't know, won't let myself know, and then I'm running down the hall, through the kitchen, past all the turquoise surfaces flecked with gold and onto the deck where I see my baby, my laughing girl, lying on her back.

Fast Eddy's there too, bent over Dina, mouth on her mouth. She puts her ear to Dina's chest. Again, Fast Eddy's mouth on Dina's mouth. Another puff and Dina sputters up water.

I observe the hose nozzle feeding water into the little round pool. Why is the nozzle feeding water into the pool? Why, for that matter, has the hose been dragged up the back steps? Who has dragged it up the back steps?

He's watching through hooded eyelids. Daring me. A metal plate slides down over my eyes and a horrible stink hits me like a blow to the head and something long and supple slips off a shore and into the water, and then my hands are around Butchy's neck. Fast Eddy's mouth is open and the same word keeps leaving it. *Stop. Stop.* Indifference makes me weightless. I rise above the deck and look down on Dina, gagging, fluttering her hands. Fast Eddy's high stepping over the broken pots and spilled dirt and splattered tomatoes. And me? I'm calmly bashing Butchy against the railing like he's something I must break and keep on breaking.

MAJORETTE

The day they moved back into the house, Marie ran up and down the stairs, and Jesse went into the linen closet and closed the door and yelped for joy. The same old house but everything different, altered, marvellously new. Cam wandered through the rooms, distracted, hands in his pockets. Every now and then he came into the kitchen and cleared his throat as though about to speak. Rita was chopping vegetables — new knife, new chopping board, new wok — for a stir-fry with peanut sauce when she heard the dryer buzz in the basement. Halfway down the stairs she stopped: billowy white smoke, a metre deep and rising. She stared, blinked, and the smoke disappeared.

*

WHAT DOES HE expect her to say? *What?* Rita squints beneath the canvas umbrella bought with the insurance money. Everything — the china plates, glass table, linen napkins, silverware — was bought with insurance money. After the fire, the main floor of the house — a solid three story Arts and Crafts, like the house Faye Dunaway flees from at the end of *Chinatown* — had to be gutted, right down to the charred studs.

Cam's got that expectant look. You'd think he'd just asked for the three-day weather forecast. A front of high pressure, westerly winds? A spot of yogurt sticks to his chin. Normally Rita would reach over, wipe it with a finger, but this morning she doesn't move. She bought the umbrella because the blue and yellow stripes made her think of Crete. Flaming saganaki, one fork between them, feeding each other small mouthfuls. How many years since she and Cam drank retsina on that seaside patio (thirteen? fourteen?), since they drunkenly tried to describe the (ineffable?

resplendent?) light as it changed through the long afternoon? Deciding there were no words to describe the Aegean light.

Cam glances at his watch as Rita walks to the middle of the deck. Why so surprised? she thinks. Haven't I been expecting this? On some level, somewhere deep in my bones, haven't I been anticipating this conversation for months? Haven't I watched it come right at me? She stands erect and lifts a foot, folds it across the opposite thigh. "Well . . . who is it?" She inhales and lifts both arms, raising them above her head. She presses her palms together.

"Please," Cam says. "Could you please sit down." He looks pained, as though Rita is causing him grief and not the other way round. "We don't need to make this harder than it already is." She holds her position for several breaths then lowers her arms and plants both feet side by side. Cam shakes his head. "It's not something we can work out, that's all I know. It's beyond us this time. It's beyond me."

Work and marriage, marriage and work. "What's to work on?" Rita used to say to friends. "You love someone or you don't." Such callowness, such smugness. At eight in the morning the idea of work suddenly strikes her as good old-fashioned sense. For the sake of everyone, she'd welcome the opportunity to dig and haul and sweat and blister. Give me a rake, she thinks, a field of stones.

She lifts her other leg. "Someone I know?" How callous and brittle she sounds. Words like broken glass.

"I'm not sure that's relevant right now." Cam's thumb rubs the rim of his mug, the nail that won't grow in properly.

"No? Then pray tell what is?"

"The point is, this is not a passing thing."

Cam works in an office with five other lawyers. Three are women. There are also two secretaries. One is a year away from retiring; the other has an autistic child and a sexy walk. Rita knows all five women personally and therefore discounts them. Though probably she should not. Cam opens his mouth and something small and dark — a junco? — flies out the hole in the birdhouse. He begins to speak haltingly.

"Last weekend. We were buying those lake trout. At the market. We ran into her. It was rather awkward, if you recall. I introduced you. Her name is Chloe."

Chloe, Rita thinks, and someone lithe and lovely passes through her mind, someone like the young woman who slinks drowsily into the early-bird class three mornings a week wearing loose velour pants. "Ah, yes," Rita says, "I remember." And then she laughs, the deep throaty laugh of a woman enjoying herself at a cocktail party, a woman who's got things to say and enjoys hearing herself say them. A woman who, above all, isn't thrown by life's unexpected punches; who, after being knocked on her back, gets right back up. "We were going to call Jesse that," she says.

"Were we?"

Even in a suit and tie Cam looks like a cowboy. His bow legs and big knuckles. And that mustache. When did he grow that? He knows she hates mustaches.

"That's it, then?" Rita says. "That's all you've got to say?"

"Don't be like this, Rita, you know as well as I do this isn't about Chloe. It's about us. Things had gone pretty sour between us even before the fire."

"I used to wear a perfume called Chloe. You bought it for me in the duty free shop on the way back from France." Cam runs his fingers through his hair, then shakes his head. He does this a lot. "I liked that perfume," she says, "until it started giving me headaches."

"Look, I should be at the office. We'll talk later, when I get home. I just wanted to get it out in the open."

"Of course. That way Rita's hysterics will be conveniently spent by the time the girls get back."

"You said that, not me."

A door slams and the tiny Pomeranian in the next yard starts to bark. "Stop that, stop that, stop that," their neighbour shrieks. Not so long ago, Cam and Rita would have rolled their eyes and smiled at each other — *Bonkers* — but now they look across the table just as they've looked across countless tables in their years together. The distance between them is the distance between stars.

*

A SINGLE PHRASE kept going through Rita's mind: *A beautiful day for a disaster.* It was the height of spring, blue sky, light aromatic breeze.

Even the garbage men gripping the bars at the sides of their trucks seemed to bend like acrobats in the perfumed air. Twelve hundred degrees. The heat cracked the windows. Smoke oozed from the seams and mushroomed beneath the rafters, but the flames were strangely invisible. Rita stood on the boulevard thinking: This isn't happening. This kind of thing doesn't happen to me. To other people maybe, but not to me.

Three fire engines, an ambulance, a crowd drawn from all over the neighbourhood. It was quite a spectacle. Hunched beneath their equipment, the firemen took long simian strides across the lawn, slick yellow apes moving in slow motion and armed with pointed weapons. Men who only minutes before had been drinking coffee in their station house were now working valiantly to douse the flames and save Rita and Cam's house. You had to admire them. She did admire them. From inside a bubble of calm she watched, as though none of it were happening. Or if it were, it was happening elsewhere, in someone else's unfortunate life.

∗

THE MORNING BRIMS with possibility. Mornings do. After Cam pulls out of the driveway, Rita continues in the deck chair, arms and legs numb. It feels as though a deranged dentist has stuck needles into all her muscles. When she was little, Marie wrote a list of ten wishes. At the top: two mornings in each day. But what else had she wished for? That Jesse play with her own friends and not horn in on Marie's? That Cam and Rita be nicer to each other. Around then, Jesse and Marie also made signs — LOVE HAS FAILED — and whenever Cam and Rita fought, they'd put duct tape over their lips, hang the signs around their necks and march around the house. Had love failed? Even then? Had it been failing incrementally ever since?

The neighbourhood comes slowly alive. Envelopes swim through door slots, splash over hardwood floors. There's the slow hiss of dishwashers filling with water. A baby cries, someone reaches to pick up a newspaper. Rita imagines she can hear a slug at the far end of the garden slithering over a cabbage leaf. What did Cam mean by *involved?*

How involved? She'd been so stunned by his confession she hadn't really understood. Was he asking for a separation, a divorce? Or was it just his mealy-mouthed roundabout way of telling her he was in over his head? That he was having an affair. Christ, what a word! *A fair.* You'd think it was a party. Let's invite everyone we know.

Rita assumed she and Cam had reached an age of wisdom and maturity, she'd assumed the late-night, maudlin, wine-fuelled discussions about jealousy and ownership and who had the right to fuck whom were behind them. *Assumed,* Rita thinks, there's the rub. She remembers Cam once saying, "No one wants to admit it, but fidelity's just playing by the rules."

"Are you serious?" she'd said.

"There were kids who played by the rules and kids who didn't. Think about it Rita, who'd you like playing with?"

She did think about it. She thought about it for days.

Last month, Cam's birthday fell on a Sunday. Rita wanted to rent an antique Chevy and drive up to Shawnigan Lake for a picnic with the girls, but Jesse had a soccer game and Marie had plans to meet friends at the new skateboard park.

"Tabletops," she said, "and grind rails. A mini ramp."

After Cam opened his cards and gifts, the girls kissed him on the cheek, then left. Cam paced the suddenly empty house, swatting the air with a rolled-up newspaper, and Rita thought: He's feeling neglected, the unloved father. She suggested they take out the canoe.

The river was full of kayaks and dinghies, people lying back or paddling madly, hats pulled down over foreheads. A child stood up in a rowboat, waving his arms at the low flying geese. After a while Cam and Rita pulled in their oars and floated aimlessly. She brought out sandwiches and seltzers. Clouds blocked the sun, darkening the water, and then the clouds moved on. They didn't talk much, but they were attentive to each other. Later, Rita's shoulder ached, and she realized how long it had been since she'd used a paddle, how long since she and Cam had done anything together, just the two of them.

And now this interloper.

What had he actually said at the fish market? "Chloe, this is my wife, Rita. Rita, this is my lover, Chloe." She *was* young — thirty something — and smiled a lot. Rita vaguely remembers nice teeth, quick flitting movements. They'd been in a rush to buy dinner ingredients — Rita's sister and husband had phoned unexpectedly to say they were passing through Vancouver on their way to Whistler — and Rita hadn't thought to ask Cam how he knew the smiling young woman — a client, a client's daughter? Later, drinking coffee on the deck, her sister had told a joke about a miserable old couple, who, when asked why they're staying together, say they're waiting until their children die.

Rita laughed. Had Cam?

*

AFTER JESSE AND Marie were born, a year apart, Rita quit selling real estate. To get back in shape she started taking yoga at the local community centre. She got hooked on the workout; her coordination and muscle strength improved. She became such a devotee she was occasionally asked to fill in for the regular instructors. And then Rita was asked to teach her own beginner's course. Up front, she told her students she drank and occasionally smoked, she ate red meat and drove an SUV. In other words, she wasn't enlightened. Most people giggled, a few squirmed. She told her class she could teach basic breathing and a flexible body, but if they were interested in the spiritual side of things, they'd have to go elsewhere. A small brown man rolled up his mat and left the room, looking, Rita thought, a little like a dejected Gandhi.

She places her hands on either side of the teapot. The thick black scribbling on eggshell ceramic looks like a child's scrawl. Jesse says the teapot's alive. A kind of Aladdin's Lamp, a genie inside. Rita's heard her ask it questions. "Who will I be if I'm not Cam's wife?" she asks the teapot now.

Inside the bedroom's walk-in closet, she runs a finger across his beautiful suits. After the fire he was the best-dressed personal injury lawyer in town. She's heard stories of women cutting up their husbands' clothes or slashing their cars' leather upholstery. An elderly woman to whom Rita'd once sold a waterfront condo told Rita she'd sewn raw shrimp into the hem of her husband's bedroom drapes. The stench confounded him for months.

The hall clock rings ten times, its ponderous gong reverberating up through the dark panelled stairway. Rita pulls out a suitcase, opens it on the bed, and starts throwing in clothes. She imagines a camera watching from above: shot of the devastated wife running away. But why is she running away? She and Cam aren't a miserable old couple. Last month they went canoeing. They ate tuna sandwiches out on the water. They drank mango seltzers.

*

SHE'D BEEN STANDING on her head when she first smelled smoke. Her first thought: someone's burning incense. But the girls were at school; Cam was at work. Rita brought her legs down, one at a time, then stood upright, hand on the wall while the blood rushed from her head. The doorbell rang and rang, and then someone was hammering on the door. A not-too-subtle early morning break-in? By the time she got downstairs no one was on the doorstep and unrecognisable popping sounds were coming from the kitchen.

"How could you be so stupid?" Cam said later. "Oxygen feeds fire, you don't give it more." She knew that, of course. At the beginning of each class she'd say, "The lungs are bellows which stoke the fires of life, the richer the supply of oxygen, the more vigorous the fire." She tried to explain to Cam that the sight of flames leaping up up up, scorching the ceiling, wiped her mind clean. Her only thought was: clear the air. Outside, Rita turned on the tap, but by the time she'd dragged the hose up the back steps and into the kitchen, the water pressure had mysteriously died. She watched water trickle from the nozzle in her hand while all around her jars of nuts and raisins and porridge oats exploded like glass bombs. She dropped the hose and walked out of the house.

*

A FULL TANK of gas, Lucinda Williams' gravelly voice on the CD player, a bag of potato chips between her thighs. Rita pulls onto the highway. Movement as sedative, speed as drug. She drives east over the Coquihalla, without a plan or destination, pushing the limit, passing everything in sight. There's a turbulence in her body, a grinding roar. Hurt, anger, release? That it's Cam and not she who's unleashed this latest cataclysm upon them? Three days, she thinks, to sort myself out. Three days until Jesse and Marie return from camp. She tries to imagine their faces but can't.

Girls, I'm afraid we have something to tell you.

Waiting in line at the tollbooth, Rita notices a group of kids moving through the foot passenger gate with packs on their backs. A small boy with bright copper curls, no more than five, slides out of a silver Volvo, walks through the gate, then gets into a black Pathfinder on the other side. What's going on? And then she realizes: it's Friday afternoon! The kids are going from Mum's to Dad's or Dad's to Mum's, dual custody, the weekend switchover, and nobody pays the toll.

Around Kelowna, Rita decides to head south. Later, entering Osoyoos, she feels a hot dry wind blowing off the land. She drives slowly down the main street, looking from side to side, disoriented. Why the carnival atmosphere? What's the occasion? The sidewalks are teeming with kids holding balloons, tourists in straw hats and garish floral clothes. Rita stops at an intersection and a couple of girls spinning old-fashioned parasols skip past. There's the smell of hot dogs and corn cobs. Mimes and musicians perform on every corner.

The young woman at the desk of the Lakeview Motel is painting her fingernails. After Rita signs in, she tosses Rita a key. "Enjoy," the woman says, and Rita growls to herself. Such a facile remark. Inside her room, she stands for a long moment watching light ricochet off the ochre walls. Hard mute walls, beautiful as rock faces. On the advice of an interior decorator Rita had had all the rooms painted vibrant, fashionable colours, colours which now seem foolishly optimistic and even pretentious.

It's past seven and still hot. In her bathing suit she walks the beach, a towel around her shoulders, passing children playing beneath a pink concrete octopus. Its face looks insane. Like something that's crawled out of the lake after a billion lonely years of talking to itself.

In the roped-off area, she plows back and forth, left foot slamming the water every few metres in an uncoordinated kick. Seadoos and speedboats pulling waterskiers criss-cross the lake. When Rita tires of the breaststroke she rolls onto her back and looks up at the sky, re-minding herself to breathe, to breathe, for god's sake, breathe. And then she dives once more to the bottom of the lake and pushes forward, as far as her lungs will carry her, and when she emerges, she's facing a squat old couple walking into the water, holding hands like a couple of kindergarten kids. Belly rolls, leathery brown skin, shocking white hair. The kind of people who, after years of cohabitation, have come to look alike. The kind of liberated old people she and Cam saw on French beaches, often naked.

*

WHILE THE HOUSE was being rebuilt they rented a small furnished apartment nearby. It had an electric kettle, a frying pan. The girls shared a windowless room. Rita and Cam slept in the communal liv-ing area on a lumpy hide-a-way couch. The old fridge hummed nois-ily in the corner, its motor kicking in and out all night. Sleep was impossible.

Rita cancelled her classes at the community centre and spent her days shopping. There was so much to buy. She drew up a sixty-page list and checked things off as she went: computers, beds, sideboards, pi-ano, lamps, curtains, telephones, stereos, pots, pans, TVs, candlesticks, pepper grinder, snowboards, towels, quilts, clothes, waste baskets, food processor, vases, bikes, cameras, pillows, knives, blender, boots, sewing box, wineglasses, guitar, camping equipment, toolbox, tools. The list went on and on and on. Fortunately, Cam and Rita's policy was a good one. Everything destroyed or even slightly smoke-damaged could be replaced, no questions asked. The sales clerks in three department stores knew Rita by name but called her The Fire Lady.

In those first weeks she was convinced people could smell her, that the acrid smoke had permanently altered her chemical make up. Strangers on escalators or in checkout lines sought her out and told her their own fire stories. She could have written a book, all the tragedies and near-tragedies. Every time she opened a newspaper it seemed her eyes were drawn to another fire-related horror. *Mohammed Iqbal, 34, a London shopkeeper, and his eight-month-old twins were trapped by flames in an upstairs room.* Rita read that Mohammed's wife ran barefoot into the street, screaming, *"Please save my babies."*

During the day Rita tried not to think about how it might have gone if the coffee maker had malfunctioned a couple of hours earlier, if it had burned through the counter when she and Cam and the girls were still asleep.

At night there were the dreams.

Jesse and Marie lying unconscious in the girls' washroom of Rita's elementary school and there's only time to drag one of them up the stairs before the whole building combusts. Or, Rita is walking down a smoky corridor opening doors. She doesn't know what she's looking for until she opens the last one and Marie falls forward, dead, into Rita's arms. Or, Rita is laying pieces of yellow notepaper (stepping stones, the yellow brick road?) across a stream. Too late she notices swirling rainbow colours on the oily surface. Just as Jesse puts down a foot, the pieces of paper ignite and she's swallowed up in water and flame.

Cam dealt with the insurance claim, often stopping at the adjusters on the way home from work to negotiate details. Rita would pick up pizza or sushi and they'd eat on a card table which they'd fold up after dinner. Then the girls would do their homework in front of the TV while Cam and Rita walked the few blocks to the other side of the park to see how the reconstruction was going, arguing about who was responsible for dealing with what.

Sometime in September the contractor phoned to say one of his guys had ripped up the linoleum in the back bedroom, but if Cam and Rita wanted hardwood, they'd have to scrape the glue off themselves. "That shit'll fuck up the sander," he said. "It's your decision." Rita forgot about the linoleum and glue until later that evening when she and Cam stopped at the house on their way back from Meet-the-Teacher Night.

"We're here now," he said, "let's do it."

They found some putty knives and stripped down to their underwear. It wasn't a big room but the black glue had penetrated the grain. For several hours they worked on their knees in silence, and when the light disappeared, Cam said, "It's the best we can do." Rita agreed. That's when Cam backed her against the wall and began kissing her, his mouth hard and stale. They'd had no privacy in the apartment for months, but his urgency took her by surprise. It frightened her. Walking back to the apartment, she felt raw and used somehow, and at first didn't hear him say he was going to *Kilshaw's* the following evening to bid on an antique light fixture for the dining room.

"But we have one," she said. "I bought it at *Chintz,* remember? I showed it to you."

"That," Cam said, "is a piece of crap."

"You said you liked it."

"I've changed my mind," Cam said. "Last time I checked it was still legal."

*

RITA LIES on top of the motel bed, legs together, toes pointed. "What do you mean by involved?"

"Where are you?" Cam shouts. "Christ. I've been calling everyone."

She holds the phone away from her head.

"I mean it's serious," he says. "I mean you need to get back here. We need to deal with this like adults."

"Aren't you always saying adults don't have any fun." Rita raises her legs, swinging them back past her head, raising her hips up off the mattress.

"Rita."

"Yes."

"No one meant for this to happen."

She walks her toes out from her head, curls them under and pushes back on her heels. "Odd how it keeps happening," she says. "Not just to you and me but to people everywhere. And then the poor kids end up shuffling back and forth through a tollbooth."

"Tollbooth?"

"Are you going to tell Jesse and Marie?"

"They need to be told."

"I can't, I won't."

"Are you standing on your head?"

"Not exactly."

"What I was trying to tell you is that she, Chloe, dealt with our claim."

Rita's neck and abdominal area are so compressed it's difficult to speak. "Hang on, this is going to take a sec. You're telling me you're fucking the adjuster?"

"What *are* you doing?"

"Trying to breathe."

"I spoke with her every day last summer. It was a difficult time and she was very understanding. Our lives were thrown inside out. You don't see a thing like this coming until it's right in your face."

Rita lifts her legs, keeping them close to her body and rolling back down. "So-o-o, what you're saying is you're fucking the adjuster?"

"No, not the adjuster. Christ, you met him. Chloe works for him."

Rita rolls out slowly, lowering her legs onto the bed. She exhales. "Oh, that's not so bad, then. She's just the adjuster-in-training."

"Something like that."

Neither Cam nor Rita speaks and then he says, "Remember walking through the house after the fire?"

"Marie's sunglasses had melted to a table."

"I kept thinking, Death has walked through these rooms. Death with a capital D. I kept thinking: Death. Death. Death."

"Very dramatic, Cam, but you're not writing a play here."

"I understood some things that day. I understood that we, you and I, were at some kind of crossroads — no, more of a dead end. I want delight in my life again, Rita. Don't you want that too?"

"And Jesse and Marie," Rita says, "what do they want?"

"I don't recall you being so concerned about Jesse and Marie when you were fucking that X-ray technician or whatever the hell he was."

The X-ray technician. Rita's quiet for a moment, remembering, not the man but herself, the way she shone during those dreadful, exhilarating months of lies. It was almost embarrassing the way she shone, and if it weren't the most sincere sex she'd ever had, it was certainly the most happily animal. She thinks back to the night she and Cam scraped the bathroom floor, both of them damp and filthy and standing on a pile of toxic crud. The heartlessness of it. And then the months of hallucinations that followed their return to the house. She'd turn a corner to enter a room, any room, and there it would be — smoke, white and unnatural-looking, like cumulous clouds on a sunny day.

"Look," Cam says, "when we've got things sorted out, I think we should put the house on the market. It'd be best to put all this fire business behind us. For both of us to move on."

Sell the house? The house they bought even though it was beyond their means. Bought in April because — ironically, it occurs to Rita now — they fell in love with the fire roaring in the big brick fireplace in the foyer.

House the girls were born in.

House they almost died in.

House that rose from the ashes.

"Rita? Are you there? Rita?"

She hangs up the phone. After turning off the air conditioner, she drops to the floor and rocks on hands and knees. Her head falls forward like a heavy dark bell. Slowly, she lifts it up while arcing her back. Eyes on the ceiling, she sticks out her tongue as far as it will go. She holds this pose as the ochre room heats up quickly and words stutter to the surface. *Blocked energy. Emotional catharsis. The great surprise of tears.*

*

Rita sits on a high chrome stool in the Cactus and orders a whiskey, neat. She tells the bartender, a middle-aged man with Buddy Holly glasses and a long Romanesque nose, that she doesn't like hard alcohol, the burning in the throat, mostly, but there's a time and place for everything. The bartender nods and puts out a bowl of mixed nuts.

The bar is full of happy tourists with flaming pink skin. A group of young women is eying the lone guy playing pool in the corner, and over by the jukebox the old couple Rita passed earlier walking into the lake, lean into their little table, engrossed in conversation, white heads touching. Rita doodles on a paper napkin. She writes: *Reasons to live in the desert: prickly pear, coyote, lupine, red-tailed hawk, golden aster. Cheap real estate. Sun, sun, sun.* She draws a round ball. Many spokes. The old man gets up and punches in a number. Hank Williams. He must be in his seventies. And then he's standing beside Rita in a shirt with real shells for buttons, reeking of some kind of aftershave. He's asking the bartender for two brandies, nightcaps for him and his lovely consort.

"Up from Santa Cruz," the bartender tells Rita after the man returns to his table. "The old guy tells me they're on their honeymoon. Me, I'd rather be boiled in hot acid."

Rita laughs. "Sorry," she says, "hot acid isn't funny."

"Neither was my ex."

Rita finishes her whiskey and puts a twenty dollar bill on the bar. As she passes the jukebox, the old woman says, "Sweet dreams, honey."

"You too," Rita says, pushing through the swinging doors of the Cactus and into the hot night air. It's past midnight and the street's empty of traffic. She looks around at the low pastel buildings, the palm trees and flashing neon signs, and it feels like she's standing on a sidewalk in a California beach town in the fifties. Any moment now a marching band will turn the corner and head down the main drag. A marching band, she thinks, remembering the crepe Halloween costume her mother bought when she was six. The paper dress that was bulky and staticky on top of her clothes, that stuck to her leotards. She sat in her desk, holding her cardboard baton, knowing she looked ridiculous and nothing like the smiling girl on the box. While her teacher went up and down the rows, Rita repeated *majorette* to herself, but when it was her turn to stand and declare herself, she drew a blank. What was she? Who? She had no idea.

A sharp-finned convertible pulls out of a gas station and drives toward the Cactus, stopping to idle at the intersection beside the Dairy Queen. To the east, above the lake, strips of deep purple flay the sky. Delight, Rita thinks, he wants delight. Well, don't we all. The light changes and the car continues toward her and slowly cruises past.

STEELHEAD

Mick's straddling two logs when he sees something shiny poking out of the sand. He jumps down and drops to his knees. "Sweet!" he says.

His father, skipping stones across the water, says, "What you got there, buddy?"

"A gun," Mick says and cocks the hammer and blows out the sand. He passes the gun to his father who extends his arm, one eye shut. He aims at the sea.

"Nice gun," he says.

"Some kid must have lost it," Mick says.

His father pulls the trigger but doesn't say bang.

"Think the kid'll come back looking for it?" Mick says.

"No se," his father says.

"I could put it back in the same place," Mick says. You know, with a bit of gun sticking out."

"Could do," his father says.

"But some other kid might find it."

"A problem all right."

"Not the kid who lost it."

"Uh huh."

"And then that kid would have the gun."

Mick's father nods.

"The wrong kid."

"Right."

*

MICK AND HIS FATHER often comb the beach together. Walking along Gonzales today, they both agree the gun is the best thing they've ever found. Mick points the gun at cats skulking across lawns, birds twittering in trees. Bang, bang, bang. He sucks the saliva back into his mouth and in a sputtering rush tells his father how much he loves guns.

"Me too," his father says, "when I was a kid."

Mick's so happy he runs up to a teenage girl and shoves the gun in her stomach. The girl slaps the gun out of Mick's hand and it bounces on the pavement. She scoops up her little dog and gives Mick's father a dirty look.

"Freak," she says. "Put your kid on a leash why don't you."

*

EVERY FRIDAY AFTERNOON Mick's father drives down from Campbell River to spend the weekend with Mick. They stay in Jim's rec room. This is part of the joint custody arrangement. Mick's mother argued at first. Why couldn't Mick's father just pick Mick up in the morning and drop him off at night, but Mick's father said, No, he wanted Mick's to be the last face he saw before going to sleep and the first he saw when he woke up. At least for two nights of the week.

Jim's an old friend of Mick's father from his rugby days; he still calls Mick's father *Stop Sign* because of his flaming red hair and because Mick's father used to stand in the middle of the field blocking the onslaught of opponents. Mick likes to imagine the puny bodies bouncing off his father's powerful stocky frame.

The rec room is long and narrow which is why Mick and his father refer to it as the Bowling Alley. One wall is covered in mirrors and a glittery silver ball hangs on a chain behind the C-shape bar in one corner of the room. Plastic flowers stick out of styrofoam blocks running along the ledges. Tonight, Jim and Mick's father are drinking beer in the Bowling Alley and Mick is sitting on the pink and red striped carpet, dividing his plastic army men into two groups. Jim's saying he hasn't touched a thing in the basement since he bought the house.

"Polish kitsch," he says. "You gotta love it."

Jim and Mick's father are marine biologists. They spend the summers swimming rivers in wet suits, counting fish. Right now they're talking about the dangerously low stocks. Could be they're unrecoverable. Mick's father shakes his head and points a thumb at the floor.

"I've got three words for you," he says to Jim. "Steelhead going down."

Mick's father crushes a beer can slowly in his fist, which reminds Mick of something he wants to ask. Are the fish afraid of his father when he swims down the river or do they think he's just another fish, only bigger and shiny and black?

"No se," his father says.

"No se," Mick repeats to himself. He tries to stand up all his plastic men in two opposing rows. But each time he gets it perfect, one or two men tip over. He remembers how mad his mother would get when his father said *No se*.

"*No se*," she'd mimic. "What's that supposed to mean, anyhow?"

"I'll take you on a swim to see the steelhead for yourself," his father says. "Maybe when you're nine or ten."

"Nice," Jim says. "You and the kid."

Mick can't wait to wear a mask and breathe through a snorkel. He imagines fish grazing his face, tickling his stomach and feet. The unblinking eyes. His army men are facing each other now, but Mick has lost interest in the battle. He feels dull and obstinate. If only he could grow up faster. He looks at his father.

"What if there aren't any steelhead left by the time I'm nine or ten?"

*

JIM GOES UPSTAIRS and Mick brushes his teeth at the cement sink in the laundry room, and then puts on his pyjamas in the Bowling Alley. While his father showers — Mick refuses to shower in the creepy stall in the laundry room — Mick folds his T-shirt and jeans and lays them on top of the gun. He tucks his socks inside his runners, and then balances them on top of the clothes. Lying in the foldout cot, Mick breathes in the musty smell of the Bowling Alley and decides this is what Poland smells like.

And then he remembers the gun.

Mick worries about many things, and now he realizes, heart sinking, the gun has been added to the list. Earthquakes, tidal waves, the water ghosts that live in the attic off his bedroom on Eberts Street. Mick also worries he'll grow up and become a criminal. He worries that a policeman with a hyena's face will arrest him and put him in jail. At night, when his mother lies beside him in the dark, stroking his cheek with a thumb, Mick confesses his fears, and she tells him there won't be an earthquake or tidal wave, he's got her guarantee on that. She also tells him she banished the water ghosts while he was at school.

"Swish, swat, scat," she says.

Mick likes the sound of the word banish.

He hears his father peeing in the toilet in the little room out in Jim's basement. Once Mick dragged a chair up to the toilet and stood on it to see if peeing from that height would make a louder sound. It did. And then he goes back to worrying. Mostly, he worries that the gun will turn into a real gun during the night. That it will push aside his runners and the clothes he's piled on top. That it will stand up and point its barrel at him while he's asleep. He worries it will shoot his father. Mick lies in the cot looking at the ceiling tiles. Some are squares and some are small triangles within squares.

When his father comes back Mick is standing in the middle of the room, holding the gun. "I want to put it in Jim's shop," he says.

For a moment, his father seems to be thinking of something else, and then he says, "Sure thing, follow me," and they walk through the basement, beneath the snaking pipes, past the furnace and hot water tank. Mick's father switches on the fluorescent light.

"Where'd you like to bed her down?"

Mick looks at his father, surprised. What does he mean bed *her* down? Does his father think the gun is a girl?

"I just want to hide it in case of robbers," Mick says.

"You bet."

Mick looks around the shop until he sees an olive green army helmet hanging on a nail. "Can you get that?" he says and his father unhooks the strap and places the helmet on Mick's head. It's so heavy his whole body wobbles. His father raps the helmet with his knuckles and Mick asks if the helmet is made out of one hundred per cent bulletproof material.

"Worked for Jim's grandpa," his father says. "He came home in one piece."

Mick tips his head forward and the helmet falls off. He puts the gun on the cement floor, and then places the helmet on top. There, he thinks, a little house for the gun. He feels better, but not much.

∗

MICK'S FATHER pulls out the couch and makes up his bed and then he gets in. For a few minutes he and Mick talk about what they'll do the next day. His father says there's a dinosaur exhibit at the museum, would Mick like to go?

No. He'd rather go to the beach and shoot seagulls and stuff. "You know," Mick says, "with the gun."

"Then it's a plan, Stan," his father says.

"My name's not Stan. It's Mick."

His father laughs. "So it is."

In a few minutes Mick's father is asleep but Mick lies wide awake, thinking about the gun and the kid who lost it. He looks around the Bowling Alley. The silver ball in the corner is turning slowly, catching the light from the street lamp, throwing tiny sparkles all over the walls. Again he considers returning the gun to the exact spot on the beach where he found it, but then he remembers the way it feels to hold, like a real gun, serious and weighty and thrilling.

∗

MICK WAKES in the night to the sound of his father snoring, short breaths followed by long moans. Through the checked curtains Mick can see the sensor light on in the backyard. He reminds himself this doesn't mean burglars. Jim's told him many times that racoons run back and forth, from the shed to the compost, all night long. And maybe it's true because once Mick saw a racoon holding an eggshell in its paw. The other paw was trying to scoop out the goop. Still, he waits for the light to go off before getting out of bed.

As Mick tiptoes down the Bowling Alley, the plastic flowers turn their faces toward him. Mean dusty faces. Passing his father, Mick is filled with wonder and dread. How can he sleep with such a dangerous gun nearby? In Jim's shop Mick waits for his eyes to adjust. And then the paint tins begin to take form, and there on the wall — tools hanging above the work bench, wrenches, screwdrivers, hammers. The vice is an open jaw. Mick can't reach the light so he kneels and waits a little longer. Finally, he reaches under the helmet and yanks the gun out, amazed that it doesn't bite.

"Gotcha," he whispers, pressing the gun to his pounding chest.

Mick loves the gun and hates it, which is sort of how he feels toward his mother because of the divorce.

He stands over the toilet, trying different things. He holds the gun to his head. Puts the barrel in his mouth. Jabs it into his belly button. And then he just drops the gun into the toilet and lowers the lid and flushes. He jumps back, away from the sound of a cannon firing. While he waits for the water to refill the bowl, he thinks: Now it's too late to return it to the beach where the right kid might find it.

He lifts the lid but the gun's still there, wedged in the deep cavity at the bottom of the bowl. Mick closes the lid and flushes again. How many times does he have to do this to make the gun go away?

"What's up, buddy?"

Mick swings around. His father, standing in the dark, is wearing the Joe Boxer shorts Mick bought him for his twenty-ninth birthday. Mick chose the boxers because of the yellow happy faces. His mother said they'd glow in the dark and she's right, they do.

"It fell in the toilet," Mick says.

His father leans over his head. "Yup," he says, "there she is."

SLANG FOR GIRL

I t's pathetic what sex does to people," Camille said from her hammock. Rain was hitting the thatched roof in sudden bursts. Sheet lightning scalded the sky. Jared was in my hammock, the whole new length of him pressed against me. "You should try celibacy for a few months," she said. "Just to see what it's like. You might even finish a semester, Lori."

"Is this necessary?" I said.

We'd met him in the Barfly, an open-air joint on the main strip. Even before I saw him, I sensed he was there. A jolt, something electrical, ripped through my chest. We'd been drinking beer with some Australians, smoking their ganja. One of them waved Jared over. Zicatela had been a close-out all day and the guys around the table were worried about another close-out. They went on and on about it: the surf yesterday, last week, three months ago, before the earthquake, after the hurricane. Mostly they were concerned about the next day.

Lightning struck and for a moment the inside of the cabana was bright as day. Jared and I were lying face to face. There was nowhere to look but in his eyes.

"Lori talks in her sleep," Camille said. "Her weird jabberings always waking me up."

"What is with you?" I said.

"You guys must be uncomfortable," she said.

"It's okay," Jared said.

My hand was resting on his hipbone and I could smell the salt in his hair.

"Or she'll shout my name," Camille said. "Like she's mad at me or something."

*

I LOOKED AWAY but not fast enough. A tiny pup flattened on the paving stones. It might have been a pup foetus. Inside Cafecito, Camille ordered sliced papaya and hot cakes with syrup. Her plate swarmed with wasps.

"Where'd you end up last night?" she said.

I rolled my eyes and swatted wasps with a paper napkin.

"Dumb bitch," she said and washed a mouthful of hot cake down with some coconut milk.

You'd never mistake us for sisters. I am short and dark and Camille is tall with straight blonde hair which she gets professionally streaked whenever she can afford it. She's what you'd call statuesque.

I was working slowly, course by course, on a degree in Psychology. Camille was finishing her doctorate in Environmental Studies. When we got back to Canada, she'd head straight to the first anti-logging blockade she could find.

That morning Zicatela was almost empty. Sand stretched for miles in either direction. We spread our towels and scoped the beach. Twenty or thirty surfers were suspended beyond where the waves were breaking. Like a school of sharks, I thought, waiting for the next big peeler. I searched for Jared and when I recognized his board I turned onto my stomach.

"Do the back of my legs?"

Camille squeezed sunscreen on my thighs and rubbed down to my ankles.

The morning we arrived we bought bikinis at the market, little patches of cloth that blacked out crotch and nipples. At first we felt almost naked.

A man and woman ran down the beach and into waves sucking off the shallowest section of the bar. The water didn't even reach their knees but sure enough the dune buggy was already moving toward them. The lifeguard hollered and waved his arms at the tourists who hollered and waved their arms in exactly the same way.

"Humans," Camille said, "what part of undertow don't they understand?"

*

BAGGY SHORTS, dreads, a flash of white teeth. The lime green fin under his arm like something he was born with. Jared drove his board upright into the sand, then dropped to his knees. He shook his head over our bodies; drops sizzled and evaporated instantly from our skin.

"Deep tubes," he said, reaching for the tepid water bottle in my pack.

"But you dominated, right?" Camille said, and turned around, squinting up at him. "You, Jared Weston, in your seriously cool orange shorts, dominated the waves. By the way, they're hanging off your butt."

He drank the water and poured the last drops onto Camille's stomach; they dribbled into her navel.

Later, Jared and I walked along the beach to the Hotel Las Palmas. The wooden lounge chairs were faded and chipped and the patio tiles were cracked. Sitting that close, I could feel his muscles expand and contract. Only half an hour out of the waves and already he was aching for them. We ordered a beer and listened to the Mexican music coming from the speakers behind us. That music was everywhere — accordions and tubas and whiny vocals.

"I like it here," I said.

Jared looked around. "Like they say. A Broke Down Palace."

*

THE FISHING VILLAGE was scattered across a hillside above the ocean, flimsy houses built to withstand next to nothing. Down by the beach, the Adoquin was blocked off in the evenings and whole families of Triquo Indians spread their rugs at the side of the road. They'd set out candlesticks, jugs, vases, hash pipes. Small girls in braids and starched pinafores would stand by their wares and observe us warily. One night Camille and I bought little birds made out of the black pottery fired in underground kilns. We blew into their beaks and discovered the birds were whistles. A salsa band played on the street and people danced.

*

149

At La Gota de Vida, a basket of taco chips and guacamole arrived first. Camille dug in. Jared's hand on my neck was a hot clamp. A fan spun uselessly above our heads.

"Hey Camille," he said, "know what you're eating? The Aztecs called that testicle sauce."

"Gag me," she said, and slopped more guacamole onto a chip.

"I read it," he said. "The men would run through the orchards and violate every woman they met. They did it for the crop. To make the avocados grow mellow."

"Fuckheads." Camille said. "You mean they raped every woman they met!"

"I'm just saying people used to believe that shit." Jared turned to me. "Get too much sun?" He dragged a finger across my upper lip. And then Camille was asking about boards, long or short, she was asking where was the best place to start.

La Punta, he said, because the waves were makable. The competition was not so intense.

We ate our tempeh burgers and sweat gathered on our brows and ran down our backs. I stopped listening to Jared and Camille talk because, at that moment, talk seemed beside the point, an irritating noise. All I wanted was to be alone with him, down on the beach. The moon behind his head.

He called me Chava, slang for girl.

*

"This sure is messed up," he said.

"Messed up?"

"I've been here, like, three months."

"So you're liking it?"

"That's not what I'm saying."

"What are you saying?"

"I don't know."

We were lying on my sleeping bag. The sky was just the sky. The earth was just the earth. A dog howled.

"It's like mainlining," he said after a while.

I propped myself up on an elbow so I could see his face. "What is?"
"Putting it all on the line. It's like mainlining on life."

*

CAMILLE WAS RIPPING the top off a little box of detergent when it
struck me: the absolute logic of sex. I understood why people sewed
curtains and drilled for oil, why dictionaries were printed by the
millions. I understood triangles and dyslexia, the beauty of the whet-
stone. Everything hinged on one mind-bending, heart-stopping,
shape-shifting thing.

I felt dazed, a sun-struck lizard.

Sitting lotus-style on top of a washing machine, Camille stared at
me while I pulled things from my pack. The machine, going through
its spin cycle, vibrated beneath her.

"You can't stop life when life's in motion," I said.

"Sometimes, I actually think you believe the whacked out things
you say."

Socks, halter tops, shorts. They all reeked of mildew.

"These underwear have had it," I said and threw them into a garbage bin.

I didn't care what Camille thought. I didn't care what anyone
thought. I didn't even care what I thought because every cell in my
body was a small closed monastic room that had thrown its door open.

*

AT NIGHT JARED and I would make love on the beach, the air pouring
over us like a hot blanket. We'd pass in and out of each other's dreams,
earth to air, air to fire, fire to water. By morning we'd be burned up,
drenched.

But the days were empty. The days were for surfing the Mexican
pipeline.

One morning after breakfast I spread my towel on the sand, rolled
my hair inside a hat, and Camille headed off with a couple of New Zea-
landers we'd met at the Internet Cafe. I sipped bottled water, rubbed

sunscreen over every bit of my skin. And then, out of boredom, I went through the whole process again.

Behind dark glasses, I watched and waited.

Growing up in California, Jared had spent so many years in the surf that more and more now he stumbled on land.

"Terra firma," he said. "It's the firma that fucks with my brain."

In a few days he'd be heading back to the States for his sister's wedding. I didn't even have a photograph. When I closed my eyes, I couldn't remember his face.

*

It was dark when we left Carrizalillo, a beautiful cove an hour's walk from our cabana. Jared balanced his board on his head and Camille and I carried the masks and flippers and towels. When we'd walked those streets earlier, in the heat of the day, the dogs had been carcasses on pavement, all ribcages and dugs. Now, in front of a shuttered store, a dog with freakishly long legs and a short stub for a tail moved out from under the awning. Others followed.

"Keep walking," Jared said.

The dog skulked behind us and the rest of the pack broke apart, growling softly.

"Think they can smell fear?" I said.

"Damn straight," Jared said, moving close to my side. Camille was on my other side. Like bodyguards, I thought. Or parents. We walked down the middle of the deserted street. Not even a taxi drove past.

"And my mother warned me about the Latin men," I said.

"Swarmed by four-legged banditos," Camille said.

Jared stopped and put his board carefully down on the pavement. He turned around and hunched his shoulders as he moved forward, growling, a step at a time, but the dog didn't back off. They were only a few feet apart now. From that distance, the dog's face looked like a squashed boot, its eyes bright yellow.

Jared was wearing shorts covered in large purple flowers; his feet were bare. If the dog lunged he had nothing.

Out the corner of my eye I saw Camille sliding toward the ditch, groping around in the dirt. She crept forward, a rock in either hand. Standing beside Jared, she passed him a rock and they both raised their arms, threateningly. But they didn't throw. On bent knees, they tilted slightly forward from the waist — Zeus and Artemis, thunderbolt in his fist, bow and arrow in hers. Their dangerous choreography, an unspeakable dance, movements so perfectly synchronized they might have been practicing together for years.

*

I STOOD on the beach criss-crossing my arms like a runway operator. Jared was a lime green speck tossed in the surf. One of the Australians we met on our first night stopped to say he was thinking of sticking around for the winter, he was getting pretty wired to the breaks.

I asked him to relay a message to Jared when he got out in the water. "Tell him something's come up, a bit of an emergency."

The Australian slid onto his board and started to paddle out on his stomach but it took forever, struggling against waves that kept pushing him back to shore. Finally, an hour later, Jared was inside the cabana, confused, water dripping from his nose. He looked around. Emergency? He bumped one side of his head with the heel of a hand, and then bumped the other, shaking the water out of his ears.

"Camille took a taxi to the lagoon," I said. "With those girls. She's gone maybe three hours. You're leaving. I just thought."

A little boy walked past the cabana's thin walls, calling, "Sport fishing, marijuana, cocaine." All day the boy walked the same strip of beach offering this menu as casually as you'd offer flavours of gum.

Jared kicked the door shut and I grinned, stupidly. "Deceitful," he said, "that's what you are."

I loosened the sarong knotted at my breasts. All around us: children's voices. I could smell them as they ran past the window — the soap their mothers used to wash their clothes, or was it some kind of incense? It was a good smell and reminded me of nothing.

*

"You'd trade your soul for a good fuck," Camille said. "Jeeze, you are one dumb bitch."

"You like him," I said.

"Sure, I like him, but do you have to lose it over every guy you meet?"

"Not entirely true."

She was kneeling on the sand in front of our cabana while I braided her hair. I hadn't washed mine in fresh water for days and my scalp itched. I gathered up tiny strands and wove them through my fingers.

"Not so tight," she said.

I slipped the elastic around the tip of the braid and Camille turned and looked at me. "You stoned or hung-over or something?"

"I'm okay."

"Like hell you are." She flipped open her Swiss army knife and held up an avocado. "Close your eyes," she said. "What do you see?"

"Nothing."

"Try harder. Really concentrate."

I opened my eyes to Camille, tall blonde Amazon in a green sarong. Behind her, the Pacific Ocean. I watched her slice the avocado lengthwise through skin and flesh to pit. She twisted. Held out both halves.

"Want to split this burg after he leaves?" she said.

I took the half without the pit. "Sure," I said. "Let's."

*

AT THE BUS STATION Jared said, "I'll write as soon as I get somewhere."

Already somewhere was the only place on earth.

"Stay cool," he said, and picked up his pack.

"You too."

I waited until the bus disappeared down the road, and then took a taxi back to Zicatela. I'd agreed to meet Camille at Cafecito but couldn't face her and somehow ended up at the Hotel Las Palmas, the deserted, dilapidated beachfront bar. It was Happy Hour and the drinks were half price. The air hung hot and heavy. In front of the lounge chairs was a balustrade someone had started to paint white. A hard brush stuck out of a paint can. When the bartender, a thin man, appeared from a room at the back, I ordered tequila and lime juice. There were no other customers so he hung around, asking questions I pretended not to understand.

The drink was strong and after the second I sank back against the wooden slats and took a deep breath and looked around. Coconut trees, thatched huts, water taxis, fishing boats anchored in the harbour. It was postcard perfect. I could have sent that scene anywhere: *Having an amazing time!*

Beach vendors walked past holding up wooden marlins, suitcases of silver jewellery set in black velvet. Some wore huge plates draped like armour down the front and backs of their bodies. "For you, lady, a very good price."

I shook my head.

The bartender returned with another drink and sat down beside me. Like everyone else in Mexico, he wore a small cross around his neck. A young couple — Dutch, I thought — the same man and woman Camille and I'd seen being chased out of the waves — walked up from the beach. In white ankle socks and golf shirts they looked like they'd just stepped off the putting green.

"Cervesa," the bartender said, indifferently, "pinacolada, margarita?"

The couple decided not to stay and the bartender turned back to me and asked where I'd come from. America, Argentina?

If I'd had the words, I'd have told him I was a wave watcher. That I travelled the world measuring the height and force of waves. I'd have told him I waited, as I was waiting then, for the rogue wave, the one that jacks up suddenly, huge like a face.

A chambermaid called from one of the balconies and the bartender left, and then two women stopped on the other side of the balustrade. They had the composed expressions of the people who lived in the hills. The older one waved me over. A baby looked out from the sling on the young woman's back. She was younger than I, maybe eighteen or nineteen. Both women were selling the cheapest merchandise on the beach, and because I was drunk I accepted everything they offered: wooden letter openers, wooden combs, wooden spatulas. I pulled a hundred peso bill from the belt around my waist and gave it to the old woman, who, with one hand brought the money to her lips as though to bless it. With her other hand, she crossed herself: Father, Son and Holy Ghost. And then she stuffed the bill into a pouch around her neck.

"Coca," she said, gesturing with her hands and tilting back her head.

I was dizzy and wanted to sit down but the old woman reached for my arm. "Coca, coca." Her voice was insistent, chiding.

"Coke?" I said. "You want coke?"

She nodded and held up three fingers, pointing to the baby.

I indicated the outdoor bar behind me, that the women should step over the balustrade, which they did, lifting their skirts.

"Three cokes,"I said to the bartender now wiping the counter with a rag. He looked up and shook his head. "Three cokes,"I said again but he continued wiping the counter. I pulled another bill from my belt and pushed it across the bar. The women on either side of me were silent as I said, more loudly now, "Three cokes, *por favor*." Still the bartender wiped the counter and shook his head. "Three fucking cokes," I said because I didn't know what else to say; I said three fucking cokes because that's what Camille would have said and kept on saying.

The baby started to cry.

The bartender spoke rapidly to the women in Spanish while at the same time glancing angrily at me. He swung around, pulled three coke bottles from the fridge and snapped off their caps. We all looked at the cold steaming geysers, which in that sweltering heat seemed like some kind of apparition.

"*Gracias*," the old woman said, and took three straws from the box.

The young woman put down her bag of trinkets and slid the baby around to her lap. She tipped a straw into the baby's mouth but he choked and cried so his mother sucked on the straw herself, demonstrating, then guided the baby's mouth back to the straw. As he sucked his eyes widened with shock and pleasure. The old one threw a sharp look back at the bartender, and then, reclining in a chair, smiled at me and put her feet up on a stool.

I did the same: leaned back, feet up.

That's when Jared's absence entered me, and I wondered, Can a thyroid gland weep? Can an ankle? A pelvic bone?

Beyond the balustrade, something shifted beneath a palm tree. An emaciated dog, the colour of sand, lifted its head, harmlessly sniffing the air. It might have been the same dog that bared its teeth that night on the road, the night a feral animal slunk back into the darkness while two gods in a frieze stood side by side, rocks in their fists, holding the identical pose.

A BAD YEAR FOR CATERPILLARS

I t's a hole," Damien says, standing behind the bar of The Duck and Puddle.

"I can see that, but why?" Hettie takes off her jacket and throws it on the pew. Through the bay window, hang-gliders drift like giant butter-flies above the cliffs. "You've been out there digging for days." She reaches over to brush some dirt from her son's cheek. He dodges her hand as though to avoid a blow.

Hettie climbs up on a stool and kicks off her shoes. She leans forward and sips the froth in the glass Damien's poured for her. "How was school today?"

"Okay."

"Okay, that's all?

"Yeah."

"And Seth?"

"Fine."

"Fine?"

Damien opens the metal cash box and starts stacking pennies and farthings and shillings in separate piles. Hettie knows it's pointless to ask for more. If she prods, he'll simply leave the room and she'll end up feeling like the bully. But it can't go on; she's going to have to do some-thing, pull him out of school, perhaps. If she took time off work, he could finish grade five at home.

Already she can hear Tom saying, "You'll pull him out? Shouldn't that be Damien's decision?"

"It's such a big hole," Hettie says, studying the generic insect on the front of Damien's hat, its ominous eyes and grotesque grin, the bold lettering — DON'T BUG ME. Damien nods and together they watch a stack of pennies wobble and spill to the floor.

*

SETH, THE POINT GUARD, is the smallest kid on the Martyrs, the night league team sponsored by the First United Church. He's also the highest scorer. The coach is a heart surgeon and someone's dad: tall, imperious-looking, the sort of man who's accustomed to giving orders. The long striped scarf around his neck gives him the air of a private school prefect. Hettie sits on a low bench between a gum-chewing woman with frizzy blonde hair and Seth's mother who's knitting something with orange wool. The coach strides back and forth in front of the women, barking names.

Boys of all shapes and sizes charge one way and then the other. It's dizzying how often the ball changes hands. Hettie doesn't take her eyes off Damien as he breaks away from his teammates, and, forgetting himself, skips down the court, silky hair flopping over his eyes. Hettie has always loved watching her son in motion. His grace and buoyancy, arms and legs made of something more rubber than bone. Carefree, she thinks, dancerly even. But this is no dance, this is a serious game where every move matters. She stares hard at Damien, willing him to focus.

He insisted on joining night league. Hettie's not sure why. Since starting school, he's signed up for one team after another. Little League, soccer, lacrosse. At seven, he played Pee Wee hockey, skating happily around the rink, oblivious of the puck. The day he understood the object of the game, Tom and Hettie were in the stands. They watched Damien drop his stick and pull off his gloves. Somehow he managed to lift the puck up off the ice and skate uncontested into the opponent's net where he dropped it. The other boys spun in circles, too confused to react, but the parents booed.

"Horrible people," Hettie said. "I can't believe people can behave so horribly."

Not long after that, Tom said he wouldn't be accompanying her to any more games. Team sports bored him.

Seth's mother occasionally glances up from her knitting to watch the action. The blonde woman leans forward, chewing hard on her gum. Seth is running at Damien's side, harassing him. Damn coach, Hettie thinks, if he weren't strutting back and forth like the barnyard rooster he might see what's going on. Damien throws out his elbows, trying to shake Seth off, but Seth sticks close, lips moving. Trash talking, Hettie thinks. Jesus, whoever heard of talking trash to someone on your own team?

She gets up and goes to the water fountain, which, because this is an elementary school, is a long way down. Standing there, she feels suddenly ridiculous, the way she felt in fifth grade. Overnight it seemed, she grew like Jack's beanstalk. For years she was convinced people were looking at her, thinking: There goes a freak of nature. And she was a freak! Whoever heard of a ten-year-old wearing a bra and Kotex pad? Her mother had cried the first time Hettie came in from playing hopscotch, blood on her shorts.

She bends carefully at the knees, turning the tap as far as it will go, but the trickle of water doesn't rise to her mouth. Her own friends had been pretty little girls who fought each other for piggyback rides. For rides on the back of great hulking Hettie! At five foot ten she stopped growing but the damage had been done. Even now, at thirty-three, she feels like an oaf.

Dribbling the ball down the court, Damien appears confident and relaxed, and Hettie breathes a moment of relief. He approaches the basket and boys in baggy shorts and yellow jerseys swarm him on all sides: *I'm open, over here, pass.* The blonde woman beside Hettie is yelling too. But Damien doesn't pass; he stops and pivots on one foot, looking around. An inane expression falls like a mask over his face. The coach's hands form a bullhorn around his mouth: "Shoot!" Parents rise to their feet. *Shoot, shoot.* God no, Hettie thinks, don't do it, but Damien does. He throws the ball off the court as though it were a dead rat he suddenly can't get rid of quickly enough. The ball rolls into the corner where a couple of little kids are kicking something back and forth. It looks like Damien's DON'T BUG ME hat. The coach calls a time out and waves Damien over.

Seth's mother folds up her knitting and stuffs it into a plastic bag. Hettie looks up and sees Seth walking back and forth inside the key, head jerking forward, arms held stiffly at his sides. It's a gangster walk, a ghetto boy's strut.

Damien, slumped over on the bench, is staring down between his knees.

The whistle blows and a few moments later Seth's got the ball. He charges forward, an audacious, unstoppable force, dodging much bigger boys on the opposing team. As usual, he refuses to pass, despite pleas from his teammates. She's heard the coach, not entirely derogatorily, refer to Seth as a pit bull. A pit bull with a bone in its teeth.

The Martyrs lose, 35 to 50.

Hettie waits by the exit door while Damien searches for his sweatshirt. Parents and kids file past, giving each other the high five. At the opposite side of the gym Damien turns and looks up, his face blank. "Your hat," Hettie calls, pointing, "get your hat. There, under the bench." He's in a trance, she thinks. He's forgotten where he is, that I am his mother, that he is my son. In the parking lot, he trails behind her, the tongues of his high-tops flopping in the gravel. On the drive home, Damien looks out the window and doesn't ask to go to Tim Horton's for a doughnut and hot chocolate, and Hettie knows that whatever she says — You played well, or, It wasn't fair you were pulled off — will offend her son. So she says nothing.

Walking into the house, she puts an arm around Damien's shoulders but he goes limp and slithers out of reach. In the front hall, she smells sawdust rising from the basement. And then the scream of Tom's table saw. Damien kicks his runners into the box beneath the coat rack and runs up to his room. Hettie wanders the house, taking deep breaths and gulping air. In The Duck and Puddle she turns on the small TV behind the bar and catches the end of a documentary on the children of Asian immigrants. In a daycare centre, a teacher is singing "I'm a Little Teapot" to a group of pre-schoolers who giggle behind their hands. The teacher performs all the actions just as Hettie remembers performing them as a child. And then the children are invited to imitate the teacher's actions: they hold up one arm and place the other hand on their hips. One or two smile; the rest look solemn. For some reason, the sight of these children tipping their bodies sideways and singing *Here is my handle, here is my spout*, brings Hettie close to tears.

*

THE EXTRA BEDROOM was only being used for storage, so when Tom proposed the pub, Hettie was game. Shouldn't everyone have a special room to drink in? Not only that, all the paraphernalia he'd been collecting over the years would finally have a home. For three months Tom lived and breathed The Duck and Puddle. He'd come straight home from work and start scraping paint and pulling nails. He ripped the fake wood panelling off the walls, exposing the fireplace, and discovered that the hearth and surrounding tiles were in good condition. When the old Catholic hospital was being torn down he drove over and salvaged a few posts and beams from the chapel. He used them to construct the bar in the corner. As for the pew, he couldn't refuse it; they were practically giving it away.

Tom sanded the floors and mixed a concoction of bees wax and oil. With a rag, he rubbed this mixture into the grain. Hettie said a high gloss finish would stand up to more wear and tear but Tom said he *wanted* the floor to look scuffed, as though people had been walking over it for centuries.

Tom and Hettie sat on the pew and tried out names. The Pig and Whistle, The Swan and Apple, The Crow and Gate. Damien, splashing in the bathroom down the hall, stopped for a moment and shouted, "What about The Duck and Puddle?"

A few nights later, Tom brought boxes up from the basement, and Hettie watched as he and Damien unwrapped old milk jugs, brass ornaments, a bust of King Henry VIII, a pewter snuff box, horseshoes, beer steins. It was like Christmas morning. Presents and crumpled paper everywhere. Damien listened raptly as Tom reminded him where they'd bought each thing, who they'd bought it from, what they'd paid.

"Remember these, Dad?" Damien said, ripping paper from a set of wooden coasters.

"Don't let your mother see those," Tom said.

On each coaster was a hand-painted image of Andy Capp: faceless men with obscenely long noses, pursuing scantily clad women with big breasts and big hair. Cigarette butts dangled from the men's lips.

Hettie groaned.

Damien was four when Tom started taking him to the Swap Meet, a racetrack on the outskirts of the city. Each Sunday morning hundreds of stalls sprout on black top. Once, and once only, Hettie went with them. Right away, Tom got down to the serious business of bartering over a biscuit tin. On the lid was a portrait of a young Queen Elizabeth in her coronation regalia. Damien and Hettie bought fresh bagels and walked around the circular track. As they passed the stalls, the regular vendors waved and called Damien by name: "Hey, Damien, how's it going?" Damien waved and called back. Hey Jube-Jube, hey Fat George, hey Alice Bee Toke. A big family, Hettie thought. Kooky people drawn together by a shared passion for junk.

"We got this from that old German guy," Tom said to Damien as he opened a leather case and lifted out a bottle wrapped in tissue paper. The crescent-shaped bottle, made of thick glass, was open at both ends.

"Isn't that a baby bottle?" Hettie asked.

Tom nodded.

"But why?"

"Don't you see?" Damien said, reaching for the bottle and pointing to the raised lettering. "It's an antique. From Bristol. Look, it says right here."

Hettie was not impressed.

"Aw, Mum, it's really neat. Two babies could drink at the same time."

Tom said nothing. They'd been through this before. "A chamber pot?" she'd once asked, incredulously. "Wooden golf clubs held together by electrician's tape?"

Once, in a rare burst of loquaciousness, Tom had said she'd just have to accept him as he was. "Some people are born with collectors' souls," he'd said. "They come into the world needing to search out the next good thing. It doesn't much matter what it is. One way or another, everything's a collectible."

"But why stuff from England?" she'd asked. "You've never even been there."

"No reason, but it does narrow my focus."

Damien got up and went to the window. Two hang-gliders were drifting dangerously close to each other. Tom leaned a framed print of a country scene above the mantle: men in black boots and red jackets astride powerful horses. Hettie stood in the middle of the room and shook her head. "No. I couldn't live with that." Hounds converged in a pack and she knew that if she stepped closer she'd see a fox cowering in the corner.

"It'd be cool if they crashed," Damien said, pushing the window open. A gust of ocean air blew into the room.

"You take things too seriously," Tom said to Hettie. He took the print down and leaned it against the bar. "You take everything too damned seriously."

*

SHE FINDS Damien's desk — third from the back in the middle row — and squeezes into it. The classroom is warm and the faint animal smell of children's bodies lingers in the air. Hettie finds a few pins in her purse and uses them to twist her hair up in a knot.

So this is what Damien sees six hours a day, five days a week.

Where does Seth sit?

Above the blackboard, at the centre of the room, is a framed photograph of an African tribesman with a painted face and bushy hair; small bones criss-cross through his nose. He's naked except for a loincloth and the savage-looking teeth strung around his neck. In one hand he's holding a spear. According to Damien, the photograph was taken of his teacher, Mr. Kingsley, before he came to Canada and put on regular clothes. There was a reticent pride in Damien's voice when he told her that kids from the seventh grade came down to the classroom at recess to view the portrait of the former Mr. K.

A few girls on the school ground are chanting: *My grandma and your grandma sit-tin' by the fire / My grandma told your grandma: "I'm gonna set your flag on fire."*

The sun through the tall windows feels good on Hettie's face, and she closes her eyes, enjoying the girls' voices, their animated Calypso rhythms. On a family road trip across the country, she and her sisters once invented complex clapping routines to these very words in the back seat of the car.

"Sorry I'm late."

Hettie looks up to see a dark-skinned, athletic-looking man striding toward her. His head is shaved. In a pale blue shirt, navy tie, and grey flannel pants, he's dressed more formally than most of the teachers she's met with over the years. Hettie moves to slide out of the seat but, realizing she's stuck, stays put. Damien's teacher reaches out to shake her hand, and then he perches on the desktop across the aisle. "I'm Mr. Kingsley. But you can call me Mr. K. All the kids do."

"Yes," Hettie says. "I know."

Damien's also told her that his teacher is big on rules and she can see now, despite Mr. K's youth, there's an old-school quality to him. He looks like the kind of man who'd play cricket at Beacon Hill Park on Sunday afternoon.

"And I'm Hettie, Damien's mum." She glances up at the portrait.

"National Geographic," Mr. K says. "That fellow is from a tribe in the interior, thousands of miles from where I was born. I tell them it's me, though. You'd be amazed how it keeps them in line."

Hettie laughs. Handsome and charming. Mr. K's accent is reminiscent of her dentist's, a woman she wouldn't recognize on the street because of the surgical mask always covering her face. Where did she say she was from? New Zealand, South Africa?

"I'll admit," Hettie says, "you had me a little scared."

Mr. K smiles and shifts positions. "On the phone you mentioned Damien is having trouble with some of the other boys."

"Seth Stone," she says. "With Seth in particular."

Mr. K crosses one leg over the other. "Seth, Seth, Seth." He sighs wearily. "Why does this not surprise me?"

"Of course, I can't get much out of Damien," Hettie says. "He won't tell me anything. You know how boys are. They don't want their mothers interfering."

"He's a good kid, your Damien," Mr. K says.

Hettie smiles, grateful. "He *is* a good kid. He's a great kid, but he's also a dreamer, and I'm just not sure he's meant for the ruthless society of." She stops and looks around the sunny, cheerful classroom and feels suddenly very foolish. Closer now, the girls are chanting, *Talk-in' 'bout, Hey now! Hey now! I-KO, I-KO, un day / Jock-a-mo fee-no ai na-nay. Jock-a-mo fee-na-nay.*

Hettie continues, less forcefully: "My husband thinks I'm making a mountain out of a mole hill. He thinks I'm blowing this Seth business way out of proportion. He says things have a way of working themselves out if you just leave them alone."

"And what do you say?"

"I say, well, I don't know, I say it's not a good situation for Damien to be in. I've seen bruises. And he won't leave the house or yard except for school and basketball games. He used to play with a few other boys but lately, no one." As Hettie speaks, she becomes aware of the unhappiness she's been holding in her body for the past few months. She's aware of the relief. Surely this smart-looking man with his air of authority will know exactly how to deal with the situation.

"Damien spends all his time digging in the backyard," she says. "It's odd. I mean, there seems to be no point."

"Ah," Mr. K says, "the hole."

"You know about it?"

"Just that it's getting bigger. Damien's quite proud of that hole."

Hetties glances down and sees that she's pulled one of her son's exercise books out of his desk and rolled it into a tight tube. For a moment she stares at the mangled pages.

"You're killing that thing," Mr. K says, quietly.

He reaches across the aisle and takes it from her. The gesture is so unexpected and even strangely intimate that Hettie doesn't know where to look. She feels a cramp in her leg and struggles awkwardly out of the desk. Her linen suit is wrinkled and a hairpin slips down the side of her neck.

"I must look like a wilted poppy," she says, conscious of the dampness under her arms.

Beneath the window, voices rise up in laughter: *See that guy all dressed in green? I-KO, I-KO, un day / He's not a man he's a lov-in ma-chine. Jock-a-mo fee-na-nay!* The girls sound frantic as they repeat the last phrase over and over. *He's not a man he's a lov-in ma-chine.*

Mr. K, propped against the desk and unrolling Damien's exercise book, appears not to hear them. Hettie watches as he presses the book against his thigh and spreads his fingers: a dark fan against a manila background. His fingernails are pink seashells.

*

THE NEXT MORNING at the table Damien bends over his muffin, pulling it apart. It's quarter to nine and Hettie's already late, but there's still time to get Damien to school.

"Basketball practice," she says, "got your jersey and shorts?"

He continues breaking the muffin into smaller and smaller bits, examining them. "It's a bad year for caterpillars," he says.

"I'll wait for you in the front hall," she says. "I'll count to a hundred and then I'm going to leave." Hettie counts out loud, rolling her head around, aware of the creaking in her neck, the muscles in her shoulders that feel like granite. When she reaches seventy she goes back to the kitchen. "What's it going to take? A goddamned A-bomb?"

"They're everywhere," Damien says.

Hettie's trembling. "I'm late, you're late, how many times do I have to tell you?" She wants to hit her son, to slap him out of his stupor, to wake him to the meanness and danger all around him.

"Caterpillars," Damien says. "They're falling out of trees. They're squished all over the sidewalk. Mum, they're everywhere."

Rage and love tear at Hettie's chest, and she forces herself to sit down, to remain calm, to think and not act, and then she remembers Mr. K, his strange clipped accent. *He's a good kid, your Damien.*

"You are the pokiest," Hettie says, "and I mean pokiest, kid on the planet."

Damien looks up, mystified. "Time must be different for me because it always feels like I'm going really fast."

*

DRIVING HOME, past the five points crosswalk, she thinks she sees Damien outside the Chinese grocer surrounded by a group of three or four boys. Tall white buckets of cut flowers — lilies, birds of paradise, orchids — crowd either side of the store's entrance. She pulls over and gets out of the car.

It *is* Damien.

"What's going on?" she says, breezily, clicking across the pavement, swinging her keys. The boys step back. Seth throws up his hands as though it's a stick-up.

"Hey man," he says.

Hettie glances at Damien. He's done what he always does when the situation is too much for him: he disappears behind his eyes.

"We're just talking about stuff," another boy says. She recognizes him from night league team. He's the pudgy Martyr with the sweet round face. He flicks his wrist, making a snapping sound with his fingers.

"Stuff?" Hettie says. "What stuff?" She can feel herself smiling too hard. No one is fooled.

"Don't look at me," Seth says, "he's your kid."

And Hettie feels something — her mood, her soul? — swing like an iron weathervane from south to north. Clouds bank behind her eyes as she moves toward Seth. With both index fingers she begins jabbing him in the soft spots between his shoulder blades. She nudges him backwards, until he's pressed against the front of the store.

"Get your hands off me," he says. "What are you, a pedophile?"

The other boys laugh.

"Pedophile," Seth says again.

Hettie stares into his eyes, their bland defiance. How good it would feel to wipe the smirk from his face. The bell above the store's entrance rings and a couple of girls come out, wearing platform shoes and short tight skirts.

"Kid's a zombie," Seth says and rolls his eyes. The boys snicker but the girls, twelve years old and dressed like hookers, watch in silence, chewing on candy necklaces.

He's actually enjoying this, Hettie thinks, the attention, the audience.

"Mum, it's okay," Damien says. "I was going to drop the team anyway."

She turns to look at him. "No way. You like playing basketball."

"I don't want to play anymore."

Damien's eyes plead with Hettie to stop, but she's too far gone. She turns back to Seth. "Want to know something?"

"Whatever," Seth says.

"You are one sorry little fuck."

Seth's eyes flicker with disbelief. Hettie herself can't believe what she's just said. The sweet-faced Martyr throws his hand out at his side.

There's a satisfying snap as he nods in the direction of the ocean. Hettie turns to see Damien walking away from the store, knapsack over one shoulder, kicking up the blossoms piled like wind-swept sand against the curb. The street seems to rise and meet the horizon, then drop off the edge of the world.

Walking back to her car, Hettie can't see the ground but her feet on the pavement sound thunderous in her ears. Behind her, Seth says in a high mocking voice: "You like playing basketball?"

One of the girls says, "You're such a dork."

"Thank you," Hettie whispers, getting into the car, gripping the steering wheel. In her rear view mirror she watches the girls move off to the crosswalk where they fight to press the WALK button. They squeal and slap each other's hands. "Thank you," Hettie says again, then tries to shove the key into the ignition.

*

SHE STANDS BACK from the window, looking out. On the rack beside her head is a copper plate that says: BEER PROVES GOD LOVES US (PLATO). No, she thinks, Plato did not say that. The beer drinkers of the world say that. It's dark in The Duck and Puddle so Damien can't see her but she can see him, waist-deep in the hole, a metre deep now, two metres in diameter. A woman's operatic voice fills the backyard. Someone's playing the same aria over and over. It's melancholy music, Hettie thinks, the soundtrack to a life. She watches Damien climb out of the hole and lean thoughtfully on his shovel, a gravedigger stopping for a cigarette break. He glances around, and, seeing no one, unzips his fly and pulls out his penis. Hettie steps closer. In the fading light, Damien pees into the hole. When he's finished he flicks himself then zips his fly.

Hettie hasn't told Tom about the scene in front of the grocer's. It's not the kind of thing he'd want to hear. But what happens now? Seth could tell his mother who could report Hettie to the police. In this day and age a few jabs probably constitute assault. One thing is certain, Damien can't go back to that classroom. Every time Hettie thinks of her homicidal-self towering over Seth, she cringes with shame.

170

As she turns to leave The Duck and Puddle, she notices the open-ended bottle on the mantle. Beside it, a small card with embossed script. *Vintage banana shape baby milk bottle from the early 1900s. Good condition. No chips.*

Mr. Kingsley, she thinks. I'll phone him tomorrow. And she imagines the two of them sitting on desk tops in the empty classroom. The smell of his cologne, astonishing white teeth. She'll talk and Mr. K will listen, and then he'll talk and she'll listen. Together they'll see a way clear for Damien. Hettie picks up the bottle and brings it to her lips. Chalk dust drifting in the afternoon sun, girls chanting in the yard. *He's not a man he's a lov-in ma-chine.* A glass conch, she thinks, blowing into one end, breath exhaling out through the other.

LETTERS TO DANIEL

Other people move on," Nina said. "At least they *try*."

I know what she means. Other people don't retreat into the sad little shell of themselves; they don't wallow in self-pity forever. Is a year forever? Are two? Nina means other people join the outdoor club and take up bridge and lawn bowling. They wear cotton blouses, white slacks with sharp creases. They volunteer at the homeless shelter and go on singles' cruises to Antarctica. Suddenly they're crazy about flightless birds bunched together on ever-thinning ice. Look at the photos! Before you know it the eggs have hatched and these people have met a nice widow or widower. Within months they're married. The newlyweds kiss and giggle. My god, they can't keep their hands off each other. This time around they're not shy about sex. Everyone's thrilled for them, but let's face it, also a little appalled.

"Well, good for other people," I said. "I'm so damned happy for them."

"You don't have to be defensive," Nina said, "I'm just trying to help."

*

A TOAST, not to the trees, pink as cotton candy, but to the end, to the end of the end, to the job I may not have as of Monday morning. I raise my glass and the phone rings. It's Nina saying she wants to go over her wedding plans yet again. She wants to make sure she hasn't missed anything. I believe our daughter has an ulterior motive. I believe she wants to catch me in the act. What act? The act of slurring my words, I suppose, the act of being drunk. She's saying Cheri, her childhood friend, has agreed to be a bridesmaid after all, even though she'll be eight months pregnant in July, and I remember a thin, aesthetic-looking girl who gnawed on her knuckles and had a passion for unsalted liquorice.

"A fertility goddess," I say, with overmuch enthusiasm, but already Nina's moved onto the west coast weather and hence to marquees. Should she and Kevin rent one or should they risk rain?

"To marquee or not to marquee," I say. "That is the question."

Nina says, "You're not being particularly helpful here."

"Au contraire. It's just difficult getting my head around all this stuff."

"Au contraire?" Nina pauses. "What stuff?"

I *am* soused, of course. Completely blotto. I am certifiably pissed, stewed, wasted, stinko, oiled, tanked, shit-faced. In other words, darling, I am feeling no pain.

"Cutlery," I say, "hors d'oeuvres, a five-piece band, a three-tier cake. There's so much stuff involved in this wedding of yours."

Nina won't be side-tracked. "Kevin's mum's into the marquee idea, big time," she says. "Her thinking is, better safe than sorry."

What is Nina really trying to tell me? A mother who cares about her daughter's happiness would be thinking seriously about marquees instead of struggling to open her second bottle of wine? I hold the phone in the crook of my neck while adjusting the corkscrew and gripping the bottle between my knees.

"It's just that your dad and I," I say, not sure where I'm going with this. "We did it so differently."

"I know what you did," Nina says, exasperated, "but Kevin and I are not a couple of ditsy teenagers."

*

YOU TEACHING at the senior school, me at the junior. Between us: a three-minute walk across the common. At the end of the day, the drive through the village, stopping at the market to pick up a loaf of bread at the bakery. The fruit and vegetable man who'd breathe down our necks as we walked among his bins, like some kind of drug dealer, pushing broccoli and peaches. These days, I avoid the fruit and vegetable man, his infantile mumbling — *juicy wuisy appley wapples* — just as I avoid everything else in a life that seems foreign now.

There's no avoiding the kids, though, the kids who used to crowd around my desk in the mornings with their little gifts, chestnuts and Halloween candy, once a skimpy bathing suit — *My mum doesn't wear it anymore.* In the afternoons, I'd tell them it was time to kick back and free fall, and they'd break into a chorus of Tom Pettys. Now there's an edge to my voice and the kids are silent. Now free falling means, Listen to your iPods, play with your Gameboys, pull your desks together, draw, talk. It means: Leave Mrs. Padgett alone. I don't say this out loud, of course, but seven-year-olds are wise and wary creatures. And they do. They leave me alone.

*

AT THE LIQUOR STORE in the corner of the plaza I push a cart up and down the aisles, picking up bottles, returning them to the shelves. I consider a bottle of Mezzo Mondo, a cheap Italian red. The label looks like a piece of brown paper bag. I can't decide. Making the simplest decision has become an excruciating chore. Mornings I stand inside the walk-in closet, dumbfounded, your clothes on one side, mine on the other. What to put on? Everything I own is baffling and offensive. Even silk grates my skin.

Since your death, these Friday afternoon visits have become a kind of ritual. I, who could always take it or leave it, have become a weekend binger, unrecognisable, someone I don't want to know. It's simple, really, and goes like this: Friday night: Drink till I pass out. Saturday: Get up, keep going. Sunday: Still drinking. On Monday I'm eviscerated and weightless, arms and legs heavy as stone. Tuesdays my brain is wet sand. Wednesdays are a wasteland. Sometime on Thursday, a glimmer of light breaks through, and I'm gliding toward Friday afternoon and that first glass of wine.

*

NINA IS RUNNING out of patience with me and who can blame her? Oh, this daughter of ours, this competent, clear-thinking, no-nonsense, thirty-three-year-old stockbroker who buys the best of everything. I imagine her pacing the airy rooms of her eighteenth floor apartment, surrounded by concrete and thick glass, her manicured nails flicking dust off the furniture. Cell phone in hand, she's telling me she and Kevin are coming over to Victoria next Saturday. He's going to help his brother move and she wants to shop for a pair of gold wedding sandals. Would I like to join her?

"No, I would not. I have plans."

"Plans?"

What I don't say: Plans to blot out forty-eight hours of my life with a big black marker.

"It'll be fun," she says. "I'll pick you up around ten."

Thwarted by Nina *and* the corkscrew.

"Just so you know," I say, "the movie people have asked us to park in our driveways."

"What movie people?"

"The movie people who dropped flyers in the mailboxes. Those movie people."

"They can't tell you where to park," Nina says. "You pay the taxes. Some guy holds a camera and he thinks he's god."

*

I TOOK MY CLASS on a field trip to the Swan Lake Bird Sanctuary but on the bus into town realized the nervous little boy with a hearing impediment was missing. Where had I last seen him? On the boardwalk? Leaning over the railing, peering into the soupy water? I alerted the driver who barked at me in an Eastern European accent.

"You forgot this kid? Why do you say now you forgot this fucking kid?"

He turned the bus around and the instant it slammed into the parking lot, I was out and running through the maze of wooded trails. I found the boy in the nature hut, sitting on a bench, watching a woman leap and dart and spin while explaining the life cycle of the dragonfly.

When the boy saw me he smiled, unconcerned, and I sat beside him to catch my breath and watched the woman who was really a girl. So this is where all the gymnasts end up. In black body suits, iridescent wings attached to their backs.

*

THE WAY YOU'D tear all the advertisements out of a magazine before lying down on the couch to read. Your imperious manner in the kitchen. Your weird left earlobe. Your fascination with gadgets, any useless gadget. Your shyness, often mistaken as arrogance. Your sex, the way it grounded and included me in the larger story. Without it, I don't belong in my body, don't belong on this earth. The way your anger would rise up, sudden and volcanic.

That day you'd been teaching *The Importance of Being Earnest*, discussing the meaning of redemption, of all things, and that big dumb rich kid whose father owned a dairy — or was he the knucklehead son of the NHL goalie? — interrupted you one too many times. You were so generally even-tempered no one expected you to go postal, as your students would later say. "Step outside," you told the boy calmly. In the hall, you grabbed him by the collar and threw him against a locker so that his head bounced and his eyes bulged. "Don't you ever, and I mean ever, fuck me around again."

The way, even in those last months, you opened every piece of junk mail that announced you'd won a jackpot. The way, when a party was flagging, you'd start talking in that idiotic conehead voice, and when that didn't work you'd crank up the stereo. You thought you could trick everyone into believing the night was still young. You hated a party to end.

*

THAT THREE DAY monsoon. I went down to the basement and noticed water coming in from the northeast corner where you'd put up shelves. In some places the water sloshed over my ankles. I hauled out the Shopvac, but of course it wouldn't work because it was full of sawdust you hadn't emptied the last time you'd used it. In no time, the thing was blocked up with sludge. I was cursing and banging around in gumboots when you came down to help.

That night we knew some things and not others.

We knew the water was rising. We knew our hands and faces and clothes were covered in muck. And when the hose was finally clear we knew our joy in the Shopvac sucking up water in great hungry slurps.

We didn't know cells were rapidly multiplying and mutating. We didn't know the cancer was already in your bloodstream. We didn't know lesions were growing on your spine. We didn't know our late night scrambling in the basement was a sort of last moment of earthly innocence.

And then spring, the air thick and sweet with the scent of things growing, you bedridden, in constant pain, the lemony light stinging your eyes. I closed the drapes and our room became a cave we all crawled into. Nina and I took turns lying beside you, Nina singing Dylan songs and me talking. I talked because I'd always been the talker and because it was what I did best. I talked because I believed my voice could keep you alive. I talked about anything I could think of, things I remembered, silly things, Nina saying as a child, "Oh, Daddy, he's an adorable sort of Daddy, but useless." I talked about the summer we drove down to Mexico in the van and visited Nina's pen pal in Morelia. I talked about how we arrived hungry, with Barbie dolls for the pen pal, white sandals for their mother. Your skin grew cold and your organs shut down and I talked about the turkey we could smell cooking somewhere, and how you pointed to the oven, which the girl's mother opened to reveal a four piece mariachi band. I talked about those little wooden skeletons in black suits. How they grinned at us. How we grinned back.

*

DOCTOR WHITELY suggested I write these letters. He said I needed to find a way to hold onto the love while letting go. I have no intention of letting go, but I agreed to write letters in exchange for sleeping pills.

Scribbling on his pad, he said he went kapootnick after his wife passed away.

"Kapootnick?"

One of his patient's walked off her grief along with fifty pounds. Another tore up an acre of land and planted long-stemmed lilies. A couple who'd lost a daughter in a car accident moved to Bangkok and took in child sex workers and taught them to read.

"English?" I said.

"What?'

"Did they teach them to read English, or, what do they speak there? Thai?"

He didn't know. "The point is," he said, "grief is an individual thing. We all deal with it differently."

Dr. Whitely is old and brusque and wears his hair in a crew cut. He's reluctant to prescribe anything more than aspirin, but somehow I had what I'd come for. A slip of paper. Beautiful oblivion. As I turned to leave his office, he said, "I mean that now. You write those letters. Next time I see you I want to hear you've been corresponding with Dan."

∗

ON A DOWNTOWN sidewalk, Nina presses an index finger to either side of her temple, concentrating. "I can see the perfect sandals in my mind," she says, "so they must exist."

I marvel at Nina's certainty. That she believes she can create something out of nothing simply by the force of her will.

Seven stores and a mall later, I say, "I'm beat. I can't go another step."

When Nina pulled into the driveway earlier, I was waiting on the front porch, wearing sunglasses and holding a black umbrella. Perhaps I reeked. Perhaps not. The reeker, apparently, is the last to know. As we drove into town, Nina went on about the freakish squalls, rain and sun at the same time. A double rainbow!

"So much weather," she said. "I mean, wow."

I stared out the window and thought, I hate days like this. I hate all days.

Nina's peering into the window of the Dutch Bakery. "Over here," she says, waving a hand. "There's a cafe at the back."

Terrific, I think. Cafes serve wine. These days everyone serves wine.

Nina pats the booth on either side of her. "Don't you just love this place? Dad used to take me here on Saturday mornings after we got our hair cut across the street. Nothing's changed. Nothing."

The dated decor, low ceiling and lack of natural light are depressing. Nina though is anything but. She is tall and vibrant and optimistic, like you. She has your blue eyes and big white teeth. When she turns her head her hair swings past her shoulders like a smooth black cape. Sitting across from me, she looks like an effervescent sixteen-year-old.

Okay. How do I say this? How do I say Nina blames me for your death? I can hear you groan but hear me out. She doesn't know she blames me. It's an unconscious thing, completely below the radar. Unconsciously, Nina wishes it had been me and not you who'd died. Why? Because her love for you is pure and effortless whereas hers and mine is fraught and complex. I don't know why it's fraught and complex — I'm sure Nina doesn't either — but there it is.

"How could you?" she says.

I glance over the rim of my glasses. "How could I what?"

"Let Dad take me to a barber?"

"He wouldn't take you to a barber." I flip the menu to check out beverages. Coffee, tea, soft drinks, juice. No alcohol. Nada.

"He would," she says. "He did. It was mortifying. You two were always so hung up on each other. You were the most oblivioid parents ever."

To my left, an old woman is making a mess of her pie. A fuzzy red tam sits on her head like a squashed cherry and her lipstick is wildly askew. That's me in a few years, closing my eyes, aiming for my mouth, hoping for the best. A waitress appears and Nina orders tea and one of those chocolate eclair things in the window. I continue staring at the menu, willing coffee to mutate to Chardonnay, milk to Merlot.

"Fine," I say, finally, "I'll have the same."

The waitress leaves and Nina says, "You didn't notice I always came home looking like a boy?"

My hands are shaking. What is our daughter talking about? "A boy?" I say. "A boy?"

*

I miss you I miss you I miss you I miss you I miss you I miss you I miss
you I miss you I miss I miss you I miss you I miss you I miss you I miss
you I miss you I miss you I miss you I miss I miss you I miss you . . .

*

It's Sunday morning and church bells are ringing all over the city.
Despite my third or fourth glass of something dark and spicy, I keep
coming back to the slip-up at Swan Lake, the boy left behind. What
might have happened. I keep coming back to the question of death. If
it's so ordinary, why can't I get it? What *don't* I get?

I imagine Nina and Kevin discussing my disintegration, the two of
them conspiring to do something awful, like have me committed or
stage one of those interventions. Maybe they'll lock me up and feed me
bread and water. I'll cluck and hiss inside a gigantic bird cage. Hansel
and Gretel will poke me with sticks.

Not just the slip-ups at school, but all the slip-ups — the broken
lamps and dishes, the stains on the carpet. The freezer door left open,
thirty pounds of stinking sockeye. I don't remember taking up smoking again but saucers full of cigarette butts litter the house. I don't remember bumping into things or falling down and yet bruises appear
regularly on my thighs and hips. This morning on my breastplate,
where a pendant should hang, a sinister black star.

*

Twenty-seven acres of garden overlooking the sea. Circles of daisies
like throw mats on grass. Winding carriageways. Exotic trees planted at
the beginning of last century. I name each one I pass. Pine. Spanish fir.
Cork bark elm. Japanese plum. Blue spruce. One, I can't identify, is
profuse with magenta flowers that droop like paper trumpets. Not
since your burial have I stepped into the cemetery but now, on my way
home from the hardware store, a new corkscrew in my purse like a
Crackerjack prize, I wander among the headstones and mausoleums.

When Nina was young we'd come here to picnic on one of the grand family plots. The pretty, dead place, she called it. While you spread out salad and cheese buns and pickles and boiled eggs, Nina would drag me over to the little marble baby chair at the foot of which are a pair of marble booties. Squeezing my hand, her lips quivering, she'd recite the words: *Eliza Jane Mulligan. 1903-1904. Beloved Daughter Taken Too Soon.*

*

HITCHHIKING INTO TOWN in jeans and work shirts. Saying, I do, I do, oh, I most certainly do! Riding down the elevator, laughing. The Justice of the Peace, his face stern as a father's, the judgement he didn't even try to conceal. Walking over to McAllum Motors, picking up the Mercedes we'd deliver to a dealership in Montreal. That honeymoon across the country — red leather seats and push-button windows. Thousands of miles of "Brown Sugar" and "Wild Horses." I was eighteen and always ravenous; you were nineteen and a terrible driver. Around midnight we stopped somewhere for snacks and gas and I phoned my parents to tell them the news. Across the street was a billboard advertising Bedrock City, an amusement park.

"Did you have to?" my mother whispered into the mouthpiece.

I looked up at Fred and Wilma and Pebbles and said, "I guess you could say that."

"Well, that's that then," my mother said. "I'll tell your father in the morning."

*

ON A SLAB of granite I sit, then lie down, and right away I know it's a mistake because now I can't move. I may never move again. I close my eyes and clicking sounds start up around my head, the tiny needles of a thousand insects knitting my hair and skin into the grass. A rosemary bush hums loudly with bees, and it occurs to me that I am lying on your grave. That I am lying on you. What remains of you. Your remains. For the first time, I allow myself to imagine you as you might be.

Heat presses down on my chest like an X-ray apron and I think of all the decomposed bodies, bones stripped of flesh, people like you who once walked the earth as though they had forever. My mind drifts on a thread, back to a long ago afternoon when I rushed around not far from here, collecting garbage and hats, the thin plaid blanket. A summer squall had blown up off the sea, spinning the paper plates in mad little circles. When I turned to call, you were standing beside me.

"If I die before you do, and if there's a heaven . . ."

If there's a heaven, what? What did you say next? Those words could hold the answer to the universe. Those words could explain what I'm doing here, still breathing, still stupidly alive.

Vandals have lopped off one of the angel's outstretched hands, cleanly, at the wrist. You always admired this angel, the way she rises organically out of her stone pedestal, all of one piece. A crow hops from her head to arm to wing and back onto her head, cawing dryly, berating me, it seems, for being what I am: hungover and sick of my own damned heartache.

Let it caw, let it berate, because lying above you, pure as a skeleton, I fall into a thick grey sleep, and when I wake, chilled to the bone, lips burned by the sun, it is late afternoon, and I'm more in love with death than ever.

*

THE SILENCE in the front hall is different from the silence I entered when you were in the hospital that first time. In texture and weight, in its sheer unfathomableness. I flip on the French station and flutes and jungle birds are talking to each other in some kind of random conversation. With a bottle of Shiraz, I sit in the bay window and watch a man on an old-fashioned bike pedal past, down through the tunnel of pink trees. A little girl, chin held high, follows on a smaller bike. She's wearing a short sleeveless dress, its yellow sash flying loosely behind. When the news comes on — the slaughter continues in the Congo, in Iraq, in the Sudan — I'm staring at the piece of Berlin Wall you mounted inside a Plexiglas frame and hung beneath track lighting as though it were a piece of art. One of your students brought it back in '81 but I never understood. You weren't German; the student hadn't been a particular favourite. It's an ugly piece of aggregate cement. Off and on over the years, we argued about it, sometimes passionately, sometimes until we couldn't speak. I'm perplexed to the point of tears. How could we let something as small as the Berlin Wall come between us?

*

WE'RE GETTING MARRIED again, this time in a little wooden church somewhere up north, in Finland or Sweden. I know we're in Scandinavia because of the light, which is whiter somehow, and there's more of it. Your head is a dome of soft fuzz but you're free of the IV and tubes and monitors. You're wearing moccasins and a ratty old bathrobe that you keep calling Bowzer, or maybe Boozer, as though it were a pet. I feel fantastically alive. Everything I desire most in the world is right here, right now. It is mine to have and to hold. I wake at four in the morning then remember: No Daniel. No Daniel ever again. I roll over and pull my knees up to my chest. Bury my face in a pillow.

In the kitchen I fill a glass with water, then stagger through the house, still drunk, stepping over wine bottles and pizza boxes. I open the bay window and night flowers assault my senses. Under the streetlights, the trees' heavy blossoms appear to be covered in snow and for a moment the seasons are confused. No, *I* am confused. I toss a newspaper, three weeks out of date, onto a pile. You were the news junkie and yet I'm still receiving five dailies because . . .

Because?

Because I can't bring myself to cancel even that miserable right-wing rag. At some point, the dream turned into a musical. The Finns or Swedes, or whoever they were, started to sing *Gotta wash that man right out of my hair.* Throughout all of it, you shone the way you shone a few nights before you died.

This happens they say, the spirit flares up like a hot coal just before it goes out.

*

184

THE HOMECARE NURSE injected you with morphine and something else to dry up the rattle in your throat. When you were comfortable, she put an arm around my shoulders and said she admired my courage.

"Courage?" I said. "God, no."

Sure, I fought to keep you alive. I moved through those months and days burning with a cold white determination I hadn't known I possessed, demanding the best treatments and drugs and specialists. Because you were my life, the only life I'd known. I'd hardly call that courage.

*

WORKMEN ARE CLIMBING over the neighbours' roof, ripping off cedar shakes, throwing them into the dumpster below. It's Monday morning, after eleven. The phone's been ringing off and on for hours and now someone's pounding on the door.

"Mum, open up, it's me!"

I stumble out of bed and splash water on my face. Did I take one or two of those pills? I open the door and Nina, all fury and accusation, thrusts newspapers into my arms, then marches past me and starts pulling back curtains and yanking up blinds.

"It's like a tomb in here," she cries. "How can you live in this tomb?"

I sink into the couch and brace myself. Here it comes. Here comes the *You've-Got-To-Snap-Out-Of-It* lecture. The *It's-Breaking-My-Heart-to-See-You-Drink-Yourself-to-Death* lecture. But there's no lecture, there's just Nina collapsing into a chair, sobbing.

"What?" I say. "What is it?"

Kevin's mum, she says when she can speak. She's invited relatives from all over. Nova Scotia and Maine and New Hampshire. They've all bought air tickets. They've planned holidays. And his poor Grandma. She's eighty-eight!

And then Nina's talking quickly and disjointedly about the night before. She and Kevin almost asleep in his parents' condo, some guy hollering beneath the window. "Glenda, I love you. Glenda. I love you." The same thing over and over and over, until Kevin got up and started to phone the police while Nina tried to stop him.

"The guy sounded so desperate," she says. "I mean, he was hammered, but still."

I look up and see a man and girl pedal past the house on big black bikes, the same man and girl I saw yesterday. It's a surreal moment, as though I'm stuck in someone else's dream loop. The only thing different is the girl's sash. Today it's tied in a neat bow at the back.

"We had this big fight," Nina's saying. "We both said some pretty ugly things. It's off, Mum. The wedding is off."

She looks around the living room as though seeing it for the first time.

"This place is a horror show," she says. "And look at you. You're wearing Dad's pyjamas! Aren't you supposed to be teaching? Why aren't you at school?"

A man holding a hand camera walks down the sidewalk and suddenly people and cameras and lighting equipment appear from everywhere. A massive white truck rolls by, *Bright Lights Production* written on the side.

"Baby," I say.

"No," Nina says, stiffening, holding her hands out in front of her body like she's stopping traffic. "I know exactly why we fought. It was because of that drunk guy. Kevin doesn't love me like that. The way that guy loves Glenda. The way Dad loved you. Dad would have shouted your name till freaking doomsday. He's probably shouting it right now, wherever he is."

I open my arms and she gets up and walks across the room and sits on my lap as though this were the most natural thing in the world. In the blinding sunlight I rock our weeping daughter back and forth, thinking, how lovely Nina's hair smells. Nina's hair has never smelled so lovely.

ACKNOWLEDGEMENTS

For their insight and laughter I thank LFC, my writing group — Lucy Bashford, Laurel Bernard, Dede Crane, Penny Hocking, Carol Matthews and Janice McCachen. Thanks to Michael Kenyon for his skilful editorial advice and long friendship. And thanks to John Metcalf for his kindness and enthusiasm, which arrived at the perfect moment, and to Dan Wells for his care and attention. I am endlessly grateful to my husband, Terence, for support, wisdom and love, and to my daughter, Clea, for leading the way. To the editors of the magazines in which the following stories have been published, thank you: "Dumb Fish," "Seattle" (*The Malahat Review*); "Girl of the Week" (*Event*); "Up the Clyde in a Bike" (*A Room of One's Own* and *The Journey Prize Anthology*); "Garden Apartment," "Steelhead," "Letters to Dan" (*The New Quarterly*); "Airstream," "A Bad Day for Caterpillars" (*Prairie Fire*); "Pope of Rome," "Majorette," "Slang for Girl" (*The Fiddlehead*); "Hitchhike," "No Gizmos" (*Other Voices*).

Airstream by PATRICIA YOUNG
was typeset in Adobe Garamond by Dennis Priebe,
printed offset on Rolland Zephyr Laid and Smyth-sewn
at Coach House Printing in an edition of 500 copies.
An additional 25 copies were hand cased by Daniel Wells.

SECOND PRINTING:
October 2006
500 copies

BIBLIOASIS
WINDSOR, ONTARIO